Sean Tyrone

A Symphony of Horrors

Seán Tyrone

A Symphony of Horrors

MARK
RYAN

SEREN

Seren is the book imprint of
Poetry Wales Press Ltd.
57 Nolton Street, Bridgend, Wales, CF31 3AE
www.serenbooks.com
Facebook: facebook.com/SerenBooks
Twitter: @SerenBooks

ISBN: 978-1-85411-647-5

A CIP record for this title is available from the British Library.

Cover image and illustrations original woodcuts by Mark Ryan

Typesetting by Elaine Sharples
Printed by Short Run Press Ltd, Exeter

The publisher works with the financial assistance of
The Welsh Books Council

For Louis and Anna

A Word or Two About My Parents

My name is Jack O'Brien and this is the tale of how I went to find what had become of my father. There are voices here that are not my own but that is in the nature of my story as you will soon discover. I would say that everything here is true as it occurred but I cannot vouch for the accuracy of my own memory or the veracity of what I was told by others. Neither can I always say with certainty what was experienced in actuality or produced by a confused and overstimulated imagination. All I offer is a concatenation of all the above and perhaps something more.

My journey begins on a small farm in County Tyrone. It was here I was born and brought up by my mother. Somewhere in the mists of another land was the father I'd never known. But in the reminiscences of my mother I had grown to love and adore him.

On occasion my mother tells a story of my father playing a game with me. Perhaps it is my first and only memory of him or perhaps it is a memory planted in my mind by my mother's not always faultless recall of events. He was never a man who, as they say, hung up his fiddle when he came home from the pub. One evening he teaches me this game.

He sits opposite me, three cards in his hand. He shows me the first and says, here's old Harry, the very Devil himself. Not a good-looking fellow, would you say? And your man here with the meatless chops and holes for eyes, he'll be Death on his horse come looking for us all. But now we see this fine lady, she's the High Priestess and if you find her you'll be safe from the other two lads.

Then my father puts the cards face down – the Devil, the High Priestess and Death in that order. Now all you have to do, he says, is keep your eyes on the lady as I move the cards about a little and then point to where she lies. And if you're right then sure enough you've won the game.

He moves the cards slowly at first then faster and back to slow again before setting them down. I have not taken my eyes from the lady at any time. Now point, he says, so I point at the card without any hesitation. My father turns it over and sighs. So it's to the Devil you're going, my old lad.

But as I said, this may not be my memory but a phantasm of my mother's imagination.

Here is my mother, lying on her deathbed. She has lain there the last seven years since the doctor advised her to take things easy after a minor fall.

'Son, I am passing from this world and I have nothing to leave you but our few old cows and the government money. And one more thing. Take this locket. It has a picture of your own father. He crossed the water promising he'd send some money home, and he did so. For a month or so, he did so. But then the money stopped and I've heard hide nor hair of him since. Take this locket, Jack. It's all I have of that lovely man aside from you, my beautiful son. Take the locket, Jack. Cross the water and find what became of the git.'

My mother is suddenly galvanised by a shock of pain. She washes a few pills down with whatever is in the glass on her bedside table.

'You go with my blessing and that of the Holy Mother Church, God curse the bitch for what has come upon me.'

She crosses herself hastily and sends a fearful glance to the crucifix that hangs on the wall.

'The last place I had the money from was in the Welsh Valleys. Somewhere called Aberuffern. I've written it down on this bit of paper. But that's neither here nor there. There's five hundred pounds I give you. Take it. I've scrimped and scraped and starved you my boy to have it. Take it Jack. My only, lovely boy. Cross the water and find what happened to your father, only man I ever loved aside from you, my dear and handsome son. Find your father, the git.'

Again a wave of pain courses through her skinny old body and she swallows a few more pills.

'Find him and and then I can go to my grave in happiness and peace. Send me a postcard, will you? You'll send me a card from Aberuffern?'

My mother opens the locket and passes it to me. I notice he has a gold tooth and point it out.

'Your father always said a man should wear his wealth in his mouth. He was a handsome lad and kind to me when he was about. You see, he has your aspect about him.

'Now find him, my wondrous son. Cross the sea and bring him home before Death takes claim on me.'

I take my mother's locket and her five hundred pounds and her piece of paper. I wasn't afraid of her dying while I was gone, because I knew she'd never be granted that blessed oblivion until she knew the truth of what had become of my father.

The Song of the Peri

There I was a girl
In my dress I'd
Shimmer and twirl
Incensed by life
Until one day my innocence
Was taken away
I can't remember
Still
Perhaps tomorrow I will

YDERYN DU

The Landlord of the Deryn Du

Oh, I'm an old lad I am
You'll never see a lad like me
I could tell a tale
And it would chill your blood right to the bone.

That Seán Tyrone I knew full well
He had his way with that poor girl
Hanged her father too
And stole away his pub the Deryn Du.

The Ballad of Seán Tyrone

Gareth Miles lived with his daughter in a few rooms above a small public house in Aberuffern. He was proud of the Deryn Du and in his mind the single bar with its faithful band of regular drinkers was his living room, and its kitchen his kitchen, although he offered the customers little provision beyond ham rolls, meat pies and Scotch eggs. The brewery had occasionally put a little pressure on him to introduce 'improvements', but he resisted their suggestions in a polite but firm manner. Their ideas of what constituted a traditional pub in this day and age were not his and lay aslant to what he saw about him every morning when he came downstairs to prepare for lunchtime opening. The Deryn Du might not be bright but it was always clean (thanks to his daughter's efforts) and the beer was well kept and the bar well stocked. Gareth Miles knew his trade and was happy in his place as publican beneath the flaking but picturesque sign of the black bird.

There was but one fly in his soup and he was a young man who Gareth suspected of making a play for his daughter. He had nothing against the Irish or colliers in general; after all they kept the till bell chiming and the boy was polite and sober enough even at closing time, but Gareth had always nursed the ambition that his daughter would marry a professional man when the time came.

Whenever he put forward his views regarding this subject, she laughed.

'So where would I meet one of these professional men? Not here in Aberuffern, that's for certain. The doctor is married with four young children and Mr Roberts the teacher must be three times my age if not more. And as for Reverend John, would you really expect me to spend the rest of my days with a man like that?'

Gareth had to concur with her on this point. The Reverend had strict views on the taking of strong drink and often preached teetotalism from the pulpit of the Methodist chapel. More than once Gareth had felt that these diatribes had been aimed directly at himself and had skulked back to the Deryn Du half in shame and half in anger.

'I still say it would be best to bide your time until a suitable opportunity presents itself,' he said. 'I've nothing against the local lads or even against the majority of incomers for they are a necessary evil to be borne should Aberuffern prosper, but surely the daughter of the Deryn Du can aim higher in her choice of partner and provider.'

Here she would always smile a light-hearted rebuke to his pomposity.

But every night there was the boy on a stool at the bar, leaning on the counter and engaged in conversation with his daughter as she polished the glasses and pulled the pumps. He wished he could follow their discussions, but he loved his daughter and did not want to drive her into the arms of a stranger by appearing to interfere in her business.

One day Gareth was surprised when the Irish lad walked into the Deryn Du just as he was preparing to close the bar for the afternoon. He had never seen the boy come in for a drink this early in the day.

'We're just about to close,' he said. 'And if it's my daughter you're after she's away.'

'I know. At her aunt's for a few days,' said the boy. 'She told me. It's you I was hoping to have a few words with. In confidence, you understand.'

'I've my customers to attend to.'

The boy looked around the bar. There was no one but an old man with an inch of beer warming in a half-pint glass. The boy took the glass and knocked back the dregs before replacing it on the table.

'Off you go, Grandpa,' said the boy. 'It's time for your afternoon nap and besides I have business with your man here.'

'Now look here,' said Gareth, but the boy was already bolting the door behind the old man.

'It's your daughter I'm here to discuss, Mr Miles. As you have probably seen yourself over the last few months we've been getting along fine and I was thinking to myself that it's time to put myself forward. And taking you for a respectable gentleman of the old school I know the right thing to do is ask your blessing before I take any step that might cause you offence.'

'What are you talking about?' said Gareth.

'I'm going to ask your daughter to marry me.'

Gareth made no reply but came around from the counter to collect the empty glass from the table. He wiped the surface with a damp bar towel, unbolted the door and held it open.

'As I said, we're closed.'

'I'll take that for a no then, shall I? What is it? Am I not good enough for a barman's daughter? Are you afraid I'd bring down shame on your pintpot family? Afraid of the pitter-pat of peat-kicking Paddy feet about the place? What makes your daughter too good for the likes of me, Mr Miles?'

The landlord stared at the boy for a few moments before giving his answer.

'It's not that you earn your living with your hands or that, as I suspect, you own little more than the clothes you stand up in, or even that you are an Irishman and a Papist. I pride myself on being as open-minded as any man must be to open the doors of his home to the public. But there is one thing that shows me I must forbid you any further contact with my daughter.'

'And what is that?'

'The gold tooth you have set in the front of your mouth for all the world to see. It shows me that you are no gentleman but a base and vulgar upstart. It shows me that you came from nothing, have nothing and will amount to nothing. And you would like me to give my daughter to a rogue like you?'

The young man held his eye steadily.

'What is not given to me freely I shall take.'

'Get out. I don't wish to see you here again; you are barred from the Deryn Du. It is my privilege as landlord.'

The young man nodded his head and left in silence.

He did not return to the pub that evening and Gareth, who had been left a little shaken by the exchange, felt that the matter was ended and began to relax into his nightly role as an amicable and indulgent host. The hour came for him to call time on his customers and he had come from behind the counter to bolt the door when it was kicked open by the young man's booted foot. He stood in the frame with the moonlight behind him and a rope slung around his neck.

'What do you think you're doing here, you young hoodlum?' said Gareth. 'You are barred from these premises.'

The boy came into the room and bolted the door behind him.

'Now, Mr Miles. The time has come for us to conclude our business.'

He took a knife from his pocket and opened the blade.

'Into the kitchen I think, Mr Miles.'

Gareth, made speechless with fear, backed into the kitchen. The boy followed.

'Stand on the chair, Mr Miles. Easy now, it might not take your weight.'

He took the rope and hung a noose around the landlord's neck. The other end he threw over an ancient oaken beam.

'You remarked earlier on my golden tooth.'

Gareth opened his mouth to speak but was silenced by a jerk on the rope.

'It is not the only gold I have in my possession.'

He folded the knife with one hand and dropped it back into his pocket. Then he reached into his shirt and drew out a golden ring on a silver chain.

'It is the wedding ring I would have offered your daughter, but I don't see the necessity for that now. As I told you, I am in the habit of taking what is not given to me freely and besides, this is my wedding ring.'

He gave another jerk to the rope to assure he had the floor to himself.

'I have a wife and child back in Tyrone and was only looking to amuse myself with your poor mare of a daughter which I might as well now you won't be about fussing like the old biddy you are. Now drop your trousers and your pants as well.'

'What? No. Why?'

'Now my way of thinking is that they'll find you there with your old lad hanging out and jump to the conclusion you've been giving it one with your hand, the rope being there for the added craic as it were. I've been told it's not as uncommon as you might think and this way they won't be getting it into their heads there was any dirty business going on aside from your own. So do as I say.'

The landlord began to sob, but undid his belt and let the garments fall around his ankles.

'So… do you have anything to say, Mr Miles? Any last words? Ah no, I can't be arsed to listen.'

The young man kicked the chair away and went upstairs to sleep in the landlord's bed.

Crossing the Water

When man first massed it was against
Cruel Mother Nature's tooth and claw –

And now we group against the sea,
As we depart our native shore.

The crew ascend the boarding plank
And each man seeks out his own place – Now come
suspicion and distrust
As each man looks from face to face.

Although we gather in our tribes
Described by class or skin or clan,
Expanses greater than the sea
Divide us from our fellow man.

Lewis ap Bwgan, Welsh poet (c.1850-1921)

I went down to the ferry, and the ferry was there. A lorry driver was queueing to roll on. He leaned out of the window and called over to me.

'Hey there, lad. It's a fine day, wouldn't you say?'

'It certainly is,' I said. The sun was shining and a warm breeze was blowing in from the sea. The driver beamed goodwill at me.

'Were you thinking of crossing the water by any chance?'

I told him I was and the driver beckoned me to come nearer. He leaned further out of the window and lowered his voice.

'Then we're much of a mind together. Have you bought yourself a ticket yet?'

'Not yet.'

'That's good. I have a proposal for you if you'd like to consider it. You can cross the water for nothing if you'd agree to act as driver's mate and then I'll drop you wherever you're off to on the other side.'

I asked myself why he would want to put himself to that trouble. After all we were wholly unknown to each other. The driver's cheery aspect vanished instantly and an almost comic mask of gloom appeared in its place.

'I have a problem with my left arm.'

'Really? What kind of problem?'

'I haven't got one. It makes changing the old gearstick a matter of some difficulty, if not near impossible.'

The mask of gloom was put aside and his sunny manner reassumed.

'So if you could take responsibility for that side of the situation I'd be more than happy to take you to your situation on the other side.'

I agreed and we rolled on to the ferry. James, as I now knew him to be, suggested we should go up to the bar for the crossing. A man and a woman were playing cards.

'Now Jack, I'd like to introduce you to a couple of old friends of mine. This is Mary.'

The woman looked up from her cards and snarled with rat's teeth.

'Call me old again and you won't get to be much older yourself.'

'Mary does like her little joke,' said James. 'And this is Dave, isn't that right Dave?'

Dave nodded weightily.

'That is indeed the name I'd answer to,' he said, after some consideration.

'Pleased to meet the both of you,' I said. James ushered me to a seat at the table.

'Now,' said James. 'Mary and Dave would have no objection to you and I joining them for a little game of cards. You'll play a game of cards with us won't you, lad?'

'But I don't know the rules.'

'That doesn't matter, you'll pick it up soon enough. Won't he, Dave?'

Dave looked at me long and hard.

'Like a dose of the clap,' he said.

'I don't know...'

'Good, then it's settled. Mary, cut the cards.'

It was a deck of cards such as the one my father had owned. Mary shuffled them and cut.

'There,' she said, placing the cards on the table in front of me. 'It's done.'

'And a good cut it is,' said James, 'don't you think so, Dave?

'It's a good cut.'

'There you have it, son. It's a good cut, so put your money in.'

'He's right,' said Mary, her face almost in mine. 'It's a good cut. What do you think, Dave?'

'It's a good cut. Put your money down.'

'Are we playing for money then?'

They stared at me for a moment and then all three split into laughter.

'Are we playing for money?'

'That's a good one.'

'The boy's a comedian isn't he, Dave?'

'Up there with the best.'

'Funniest thing I've heard in years.'

James dabbed at his eyes and waved the other two down.

'We have to remember,' he said, 'that the game of cards is a serious concern.'

Mary gripped my wrist.

'So put your money down, boy.'

'How much should I put in?'

James considered.

'Well, let's say…'

'There's a fair old bulge in his breast pocket,' said Mary.

'Then let's say a ton just to start us on our way.'

'A ton?' I said. 'Do you mean a hundred pounds?'

'Start low and build your way up,' said James.

'You want to play with the boys,' said Mary. 'You have to show your bollocks. Isn't that right, Dave?'

'That's what they say, right enough.'

James put his arm round my shoulders and beamed reassurance.

'You'll win it all back, with luck. Count out your money.'

'There's got to be five hundred pound in there,' said Mary. 'Dave?'

'Five hundred, I'd say. At least five hundred.'

'So count it out, and we'll play the game.'

'Put your money down, boy.'

'But a hundred pounds?'

'What's that between friends?' said James. 'What did you say your name was?'

'Jack.'

'I feel I've known you all my life already, Jack. Welcome to our game.'

'Get him to put his money down,' said Mary. 'Dave, tell him.'

'Put your money down.'

'A hundred pounds you say.'

'You'll win it back. That's right, boy. On the table.'

'And I'll win it back?'

'Of course you will. Straightaway, won't he Dave?'

'Straightaway.'

'Then it's game on,' said James. 'Pull the top card.'

I turned it over.

'Well, there you have it. There's no beating the Heirophant is there, Dave?'

'There's no beating that old card, you're right enough there.'

'So I've won?'

The three of them rocked about, slapping their thighs.

'Did you hear that? So I've won?'

'That boy will be the death of me.'

'I don't know where he gets them from do you, Dave?'

'Better than anything on the telly.'

James dabbed at his eyes and Mary turned to me, her face hard once more.

'You've lost your whack. Put some more on the table.'

'There's no need to look downhearted, lad,' said James. 'You're sure to win it back. Perhaps if we upped the stakes. Two hundred on the table. That's fair enough isn't it, Dave?'

'It would certainly strike me as so.'

'Two hundred pounds?' I said.

'If you don't have the bollocks...' said Mary.

'I've got the bollocks all right. Here. Two hundred pounds on the table. Cut the cards, Mary.'

As we all leaned forward, she cut the deck again. I turned over the top card.

James sighed deeply.

'Ah, it's not good news. The High Priestess. And following as she does the Heirophant you've taken a bit of a blow to your personal finances, isn't that the case, Dave?'

'It would appear thus, the truth be told.'

'I can only suggest you put whatever money remains to you on the table in an attempt to cover your losses. Do you agree, Dave?'

'The only right and sensible thing to do.'

'But I've only got two hundred pounds left from the money my mother gave me to find my father.'

'Put it on the table,' said Mary.

'You'll be sure to win it back. Won't he, Dave?'

'It's a possible sureity.'

'Put the money on the table,' said Mary, 'and I'll cut the cards.'

'Cover your losses, Jack my lad.'

'The money, now.'

I put my remaining money on the table and Mary cut the deck. My eyes closed in silent prayer, I turned over the top card. My three new friends sucked in their breath sharply and I heard the sound I had come to dread.

James sighed as though overcome with the woes of the world.

'Oh, my poor boy. My poor, poor boy.'

'He's poor now,' said Mary.

'A sock in it, you gobshite,' said James and took me by the shoulders. 'You see… ah…'

'Jack.'

'Of course. Jack. The Fool coming after the Heirophant when the intermediary is the High Priestess has spelt bad luck for you, my boy. Dave would agree with me here. Dave? Would you concur?'

'Whole-heartedly.'

Mary leaned into my face.

'Now we've had your money, so get yourself to hell.'

I had lost all my mother's money and the only possession I had now to my name was the locket containing the image of my father. By luck it was hidden inside my shirt or without doubt they would have had that from me as well. The ferry docked and I had no choice but to accept a lift from James.

I rode in the cab, changing gears on demand. I had no wish to discuss the game but felt I should make some attempt at conversation.

'How did you lose it?'

'Second!'

'Sorry?'

'The gearstick, boy. Second.'

'Oh, right you are.'

I changed gear.

'Now what did you say? How did I lose my arm?'

'If you don't mind my asking.'

'It's a sad story, although there may be a lesson in it for you. Third!'

I changed gear again, beginning to get the hang of the thing.

'But bear in mind, boy, that once you have heard my tale you can never unhear it. Are you sure you want me to tell it?'

I told him I was.

'It was in a card game such as the one you have learnt today.'

'You lost your arm in a card game? How did that work out?'

'These things happen. Third! You throw in your chips and there must be consequences. The Lord moves in mysterious ways his wonders to perform. Good and bad. You can leave with a whack of some other tosser's stash or you shrug your shoulders and pay up. Fourth!

'I was a young man at the time, not much older than yourself. Although I had paid little attention to my academic studies and failed in the school certificate, I had laboured long and hard to master the chemistry of drink and the biology of women; indeed I was quite the scholar in both subjects, and through diligent study and brave experimentation gained distinction in the arts of dissipation. It was only natural that in time I should graduate to the mathematics of cards. Back down to second!

'But there are people in this world, my boy, who would take advantage of the curious and revel in the destruction of their fortune. Unhappily, I fell in with a group of such fellows and watched as first they took my money, my grandfather's gold watch and my sister's virtue until I had nothing left to stake. Or so I thought.

'One of them, an evil-looking rogue with a rope-burn around his neck, suggested that I might place my arm upon the table. At first I misunderstood his meaning, but he elaborated. His proposal was that I should stake my left arm; I laughed at the idea, but it was seized upon by the rest of the company and I, intelligence dulled by drink and appetite sharpened by avarice, agreed. Third!'

'And you lost.'

'I lost. Not just the hand, but my whole arm. They fell upon me with knives and in a matter of moments I was as you see me now. Divided from my limb but multiplied in sorrow.'

'But your arm. What could they have possibly wanted with it?'

'The point has been missed, lad. It's the principle of the thing. You put in your chips, you lose and you pay up. It's the rules of the game. You play, you pay. Rules of the game, old son.'

'What did they do with it?'

'Chucked it, most probably. Third! No use to them. Like I say, it's the principle of the thing. But it might've been worse, old son.'

'How?'

'Might've been my right arm. Never have I managed to bring off a satisfactory wank with the old left hand. It's not the same somehow. Now where do you want dropping off?'

'Aberuffern. It's a place in the Valleys.'

James turned to me, his mouth agape.

'Aberuffern?'

How Dave Met His Death

The earliest memory Dave had was of a little rhyme his mother sang. She sang it when she fed him, when she bathed him and when she put him to bed. She sang it when he cried, when he had been disobedient and when he had soiled himself.

She had probably sung it to him before he had words enough to fix it in his memory and she was still singing it when he left home to attend his first day at school.

He was sat next to a boy he had never met before. The teacher asked the boy his name and received the answer 'Dave'. The teacher nodded and passed on to Dave.

'And what is your name?'

'Dave.'

The class stirred with stifled laughter.

'Quiet,' said the teacher. 'Dave is a common enough name. There is nothing surprising or amusing that two boys, each named Dave, should find themselves sitting together.'

At the end of the day, Dave's mother was waiting for him at the school gate. She called for him and he ran to her.

'My name is Dave now,' he said. 'You must call me Dave from now on.'

His mother accepted this without comment and led him home for tea.

Now it turned out that the other Dave lacked the advantage of Dave's peaceful upbringing, having a drunken lout for a father who beat his mother and son regularly. She, in her bitterness, became a vindicative woman who vented her spite at the world on her only boy. He in turn, being well-grown for his age and lacking any benign influence at home, found himself comfortable in the role of class bully.

Dave would have been his natural prey but, whether it was due to their shared name or that Dave seemed unaffected by any attack, verbal or physical, he failed to satisfy the bully's appetite for intimidation. Instead, Dave became his ally and proved himself valuable whenever the bully needed an explanation, justification or alibi.

Dave's school years went by uneventfully; indeed he could have been said to have spent them profitably. He did passably well in tests, rarely scoring below half-marks due to his habit of answering 'yes' rather than 'no', and 'true' rather than 'false' whenever given the choice which, for the benefit of the examiner, was more often than not.

When the time came to leave school Dave, having passed top of the class, secured work immediately but he soon found this tedious and unrewarding. His friend, the bully, had fallen in with a gang of thieves and rogues and, missing Dave and his compliancy, had little difficulty in persuading him into this alternative employment.

Dave proved to be popular; he drank drink for drink with the best and the worst of them and was never last to buy his round at the bar. Soon he gained a reputation for wisdom, and no plan was put into action until it met with his approval. This approval was always forthcoming which added to his popularity.

Once there was a girl who showed an interest in Dave. She plied him with smiles and gentle touches to his sleeve. His friends croaked their jibes and cawed their obscenities behind his back. It was obvious to a deaf and blind cat what she was after, but Dave was amicably unaware of it all.

Time passed and the girl grew impatient with his indifference and took the bold step of asking him out herself and to no one's surprise but his own he agreed.

Dave, who had always been content with the way life had been going, now found real happiness in the company of this girl. With her the sun always shone, the birds always sang and he found a new spring in his step.

One day this happiness was torn from him when she said she no longer wished to see him. He asked for a reason and this is the answer she gave:

'When we first met it was clear that you liked me, but you never had it in you to ask me out. When we did go out it was because I was tired of waiting for you to make the first move. When I asked where we should go, you asked me where I should like to go. When we first kissed it was because I pressed my lips to yours.

'This is not what I want from a man. I want a man who knows what he wants and goes out to get it. I want a man who knows his own mind and stands by his decisions. I want a man who stands up to the world and damns all the rest. You are a kind and pleasant man, but you are none of these things. It would be cruel of me should I lead you on any further.'

Dave listened to her in silence because he knew she was right. As he watched her walk away he understood the nature of sadness and loss but did nothing.

The time came when his mother fell mortally ill and with her last breath she sang him the little rhyme that was his first memory. The tears dribbled down his face as he heard the words that had guided his every step in life and he joined his voice to hers.

When you're asked a question
Agree with all the rest
Always go
With the flow
You'll find it's for the best.

His mother was gone, his sweetheart was gone and next went his friend the bully, shot dead by the police outside a bank. He was armed with an umbrella wrapped in a carrier bag.

One by one the gang drifted away; to death, to prison, to sickness, to women. The day came when Dave stood alone at the bar with no one to match drink for drink, no approval to give and none to gain. He took a bottle from the shelf and went home to the bed in his mother's house. He started to undress, but the weight of his tiredness made a monstrous imposition of even this slight activity.

Which is how the man from the council found him a few days later, dead on his bed with one sock on and one sock off.

Aberuffern

The valley where Aberuffern now lies was originally the site of a scattering of farm houses, no more than forty in number. With the sinking of the pit and the raising of the coal by the Parry Glamorgan Colliery Company in the latter years of the last century, the population has swollen to over five thousand in only fifty years. Streets have climbed up the slopes of the valley to house the influx of newcomers and the yeomanry have forsaken their pastures to work the seams, lured by the promise of higher wages. The springs around Aberuffern have all but dried up, and where once a profusion of wild flowers flourished there remain only a few sorry weeds. The cause of this blight is the steady removal of the coal far beneath the fields where in days of yore the shepherd drove his flock.

From '*An Aberuffern Schoolmaster*' by J. P. Huntley.
(Tremorgan, 1942. Elysian Press)

'Now where did you say you wanted dropping off?' asked James.

'Aberuffern. It's a place in the Valleys.'

James drew a deep breath and sighed, slowly shaking his head from side to side.

'Aberuffern, you say? I'd steer clear of there if I was you, my old son. It's near my route but thank the Lord Jesus I don't have to set foot in that accursed place.'

'Why? What's wrong with it?' I said. It was clear that James' mood had taken a turn for the worse; a cloud obscured his sunny disposition and his voice grew darker.

'Nothing good is ever said of Aberuffern, if it is ever talked of at all.'

The driver sang; a dark and doleful melody.

> In that black place upon the hill,
> No soul worth a penny to old Harry himself,
> Carrion crows circle in the skies,
> A man's own shadow walks in disguise,
> Sorrow haunts each pair of eyes
> In Aberuffern.

The church stripped bare, her windows smashed,
The Saviour on His Cross planted upside-down;
Carrion crows circle in the skies,
Croak as the tortured baby cries;
Hatred haunts each pair of eyes
In Aberuffern.

The graves lie empty, the corpses gone
To satisfy the appetites of the ghouls;
Carrion crows circle in the skies,
Even the Moon is afraid to rise,
Evil haunts each pair of eyes
In Aberuffern.

He sighed; a dark and doleful sigh.

'Now, here it is. See those burnt-out houses down there? On the other side of those trees?'

'I see the trees.'

'They call that Coed-y-Cysgod.'

'And does that mean something?'

'Everything has a meaning, old son. It means the Wood of the Shadow or the Shadow Wood. Whichever takes your fancy. Take the road through the woods and you'll find Aberuffern on the other side, God help you, although I doubt that He will. You'll be getting out here. Goodbye, Jack me old lad.'

I thanked him and jumped down from the cab. The lorry pulled away and was soon out of sight but the melody lingered in my head.

The road down the hillside was flanked by dense woodland. As the road shrank to a lane, to a path, the hedgerows grew above themselves and knotted into a tangled canopy that kept most of the grey evening light from my eyes. It was the goading of the thorns from left and right that kept me to the centre of the path.

In the darkness I became aware of certain Things moving in the periphery of my vision. If I tried to catch one out by looking at it directly there was nothing there, but the movement continued in another place. I had the glimpsed impression that these Things were small, black and furred, with an occasional flash of yellow teeth. I set my lips to whistle, but thought better of it; I had no desire to show any vulnerability to these creatures.

Now they made themselves heard to me:

> Jack O'Brien, son of Seán Tyrone
> You're on your own;
> But we'll be with you
> As you walk alone.

Their voices were neither inside my head nor without. They had made instruments of the delicate bones and skins that formed my ears to play their intimate music.

I walked on. It made no difference as to whether my eyes were open or shut; I could perceive their movements still, closer to me now, their music growing louder and shriller, keeping beat to the thumping of my heart:

> Jack O'Brien, son of Seán Tyrone
> Bad to the bone
> We'll stay here with you
> As you walk alone.

Did their fur brush my cheek or was it ancient gossamer that caressed my face? I walked faster, the thorns clawing at my sleeves, until I saw a sickly light ahead. I began to run, as best I could. Although the light grew in size, it gained little in intensity; but it was all hope had to give me.

> Jack O'Brien, son of Seán Tyrone
> His flesh and bone;
> Forever we're with you
> As you walk alone.

The final approach to the village was over an expanse of scorched earth that offered nothing to sustain life. The voices died away in my ears as I recovered my breath, walking the last few hundred yards to the nearest house. A crow stood regarding me. I kicked a stone in its direction; it croaked a vile imprecation and flew away. The door to the house was open. I banged twice on the flaking panels with my fist and stepped inside. There was no light but a thin voice cried out to me:

'Pwy sydd 'na? Who's that there?

'Jack. Jack O'Brien.'

'Rings no bells with me. Nos da.'

'I'm looking for my father.'

'Nothing to do with me. I deny it absolutely.'

As my eyes adjusted to the shadows I could discern a woman lying beneath a blanket on a wreck of a sofa, her matted greasy black hair trailing over the cushions. Her gauntly lined face showed the remnants of make-up and dried saliva made a slug track from the side of her mouth. The one thin, twisted hand I could see shook as she spoke:

'There was no other bastard there see me do it, right? It was a dark night and I was a tipyn bach tipsy. He wasn't any too good-looking, so I thought of myself as doing him a favour, you might say.

'But then I was up the spout, wasn't I? But like I said, I had no attachment to the bloke so I thinks nothing of giving the bastard bach over to the Council to look after, a pwy yn y byd could have blamed me?

'Step forward so as I can have a look at you. See? There's your proof. You look nothing like me. Nor him, and at least you've got that to be grateful for. There's your proof. Now, nos da.'

I took the locket from around my neck and held out the picture. Her eyes were closed.

'His name is Seán O'Brien. I have his picture here. Please look.'

The woman opened her lids reluctantly. When she saw the picture, fire came into her eyes and she clawed for the locket.

'Give it here. Duw, duw. Oh I know that face, all right. But not by that name. We knew him as Seán Tyrone because his name was Seán and he came from Tyrone. Is that him?'

I dropped the locket inside my shirt and stepped back. I could not tell whether the stench of damp and decay came from her or the furniture. Perhaps they had fused into one.

'Is he still here?' I said.

'He's here. He's here in everything you see around you. He'll always be here. Jack, wasn't it? Now the bells are ringing. I have his pistol here for you.'

Painfully the woman reached under the sofa and brought out an oily bundle which she unwrapped caressingly as she spoke.

'When I was a girl younger than you yourself is now, I was told three things about a pistol. You don't carry him until you've learnt to break him, clean him, oil him and put him back together. Don't bother with all that bastard marksmanship, you won't need it. Don't use your pistol as a threat. If you haven't managed that with your eyes already, you are down on the game. Even the odds. No talking, no clever remarks. Pull out your pistol and use him straightaway to have done with the bastard, then there's no argument. He's gone and you is walking away. Dim problem.'

'Isn't that more than three things?'

'Three things is as many as I wants them to be. Now take it and go. I want nothing more to do with the man, nor any of his kind.'

'Where can I find him?'

'As I said. Wherever you look.'

She stared blankly at the pistol in her hand; head nodding, mouth drawing short painful breaths.

'Wait, son of Seán Tyrone. I have one further use for his pistol.'

She raised the pistol to her mouth and, with both thumbs on the trigger and her eyes on mine, she fired.

The flash of flame and the whiplash crack of the explosion deafened and blinded me for a moment and then I saw her face hanging before me, wreathed in coiling tendrils of smoke. Although her eyes were turning up in their sockets and she swayed upon her legs, she held the heavy pistol out to me. Then she melted to the floor, her head cushioned in an expanding pool of black blood. I felt the warmth of the pistol entering my fingers. Where would I put it? Should I leave it there or take it with me? Where should I report this?

I tucked the pistol into my belt and tried the light switch. As I had expected, there was no result. A cigarette lighter lay on an upturned box beside a candle stump jammed into the neck of a half-bottle of cheap vodka. I lit the candle and held the flame to the woman's lips. There was no breath in her body, if there ever had been. I returned the bottle to the upturned box and slipped the lighter into my pocket. There was nothing in this room to tell me anything about this woman who had known my father and I could not bring myself to search her reeking clothes. So I left the candle to stand vigil in that damp, dark, stinking tomb and left the house, pulling the door behind me.

On the street the evening light had gone. I could see no moon in the sky, but here and there objects seemed to glow with their own pale luminosity. I felt I should talk to someone in authority about the woman but none of the windows in the street were lit. I considered crying out, but was reluctant to hear my own voice echoing in that barren and deserted place. A few hundred yards or so away stood a chapel. I followed the iron fence of the graveyard to the gateway – the gate itself had been removed.

The stones in the graveyard had been pulled from the earth and lay haphazardly among the graves, most of which had been looted or desecrated in some way. The Irish names jostled with the Welsh in the ruins. Here had lain Margaret Whelan, beloved wife of Patrick, her name picked out in lead on her ruined monument above the names of the six children who had died on an annual basis from her eighteenth year until she eventually followed them to this place. Of Patrick Whelan, there was no further mention.

Approaching the chapel I observed that the door had gone the way of the gate. I stood in the porch and stared into the darkness. There was nothing; nothing but the same smell of damp and decay that had permeated the woman's house. I breathed shallowly to avoid inhaling the foul odour of corruption that hung with still menace inside those walls. There was no authority here.

Turning away from the chapel, I thought I saw something move among the stones. Was it one of my hillside companions? If so, I felt no fear. They had failed to harm me then and now I had the weight of the pistol at my belt. I called out:

'Who's there? Come out. I want to ask you something.'

There was silence, but I was aware of an electric presence, a sensation of breath held back, limbs coiled in preparation for flight or attack.

'Come out. Let me see you. All I want is to ask you a question or two. I'm alone and unarmed. Please. You've nothing to fear from me.'

Whoever was there suppressed a chuckle and I saw a dark shape move to the cover of a derelict monument.

'Listen. There's been an accident. I need to tell someone about it… I have to inform the authorities. Help me.'

That chuckle again. I could not tell if it was man, woman or child. My temper began to rise, but I tried to keep it from my voice. I walked towards the angel.

'Come out. You have nothing to be afraid of.'

I thought I heard a rustle of dead leaves, and held my breath to listen. Suddenly I heard the chuckle close behind me, almost at my ear, and I spun round. There was nothing there, but I had a new horror to confront.

The pistol was in my hand.

I stared at it, mouth slack. I held it there in front of me, searching for some kind of explanation but there was none. It had been in my belt and now, through no agency of my own, it was in my hand. My impulse was to throw the murderous object as far from me as possible, but my body was oblivious to the urgings of my spirit and the weight of the pistol dropped my arm to my side. I walked unsteadily back to the street and leaned against the gatepost.

The Reverend John Receives a Visitor

The Reverend complained and so
Without a single word Tyrone
Drowned him in the font
And under a dung pile he buried him.

The Ballad of Seán Tyrone

The Reverend John Wesley John took to the pulpit and, as was his habit, spent some time in contemplation of the assembly before delivering his address. His purpose here was twofold; firstly he well understood the theatrical nature of his calling and, like an actor of the old school, expected and demanded the full attention of his audience before making his speech.

Any cough or scraping of feet was punished by the lash of his stare and instantly silenced. Secondly, he wished to define those penitents who met his eye openly and without guilt from those whose attention was held by any insignificant object they could fix upon. These sinners would be the targets in whom his arrows of righteous accusation would be fastened.

There was a young woman seated four rows back who showed a preoccupation with the neck of the gentleman seated in front. One of her eyes was bruised and swollen; the minister knew her name and who she was. He licked his lips and gripped the sides of the pulpit.

'First, it is with sadness that we must note the passing of one of our number. A man I know was well liked and even respected by some of you in spite of his obvious failings. The coroner has returned a verdict of death by misadventure. Misadventure, my friends. There is a way which seemeth right to a man but thereof are the ways of death. We are all acquainted with the evidence presented at the hearing and cannot help but be reminded of Onan, who spilled his seed on the ground and the thing which he did displeased the Lord, wherefore he slew him.'

Had the girl suppressed a small bleat of distress just then? He paused for a moment and then continued, frustrated at her lack of reaction.

'It is hardly surprising that this man was the proprietor of one of those houses where the loathsome germ of iniquity multiplies and corrupts. You know whereof I speak but I will not profane this place of worship with its abhorrent name. It is also without surprise that this house of evil is now host to the infernal practice of fornication. Yes, their names are known to all of you here, but not only do you permit this abominable liaison to pass unchallenged in your midst but there are some before me today who continue to frequent that cesspit of drunkenness and debauchery in spite of its infernal associations. And they come here today cap in hand begging forgiveness but will surely return to their sinful ways tomorrow.'

He looked around and was gratified to see that several pairs of eyes now failed to meet his.

'Who hath woe? Who hath contentions? Who hath wounds without cause? Who hath red eyes?'

The young woman allowed a tress of golden hair to fall over her blackened eye. Yes, his words were definitely penetrating that demure shield now.

'They that tarry long at the wine. Drink biteth like a serpent and stingeth like an adder but you will say "they have stricken me and I was not sick; they have beaten me, and I felt it not: when shall I awake? I will seek it yet again." Drunkenness and fornication are listed high among the sins of the flesh. They who would do such things shall not inherit the kingdom of God but shall be cast into the eternal flame by His vengeful hand.'

Again, that suppressed whimper from the fourth row.

'So what is to be done? How may these sinners redeem themselves? The answer, my friends, is to be found like all others in the Holy Scripture. Walk not after the flesh, but after the Spirit, for they that are after the flesh do mind the things of the flesh; but they that are after the Spirit do mind the things of the Spirit. For to be carnally minded is death; but to be spiritually minded is life and peace. We shall now sing "Nearer, my God, to Thee".'

That afternoon Reverend J.W. John had several calls to make in the village; he delivered comfort to the sick, solace to the bereaved and exhortations to the wicked. It was evening before the minister returned to the chapel where he was surprised to find the door standing open and a young man swinging his legs from the sacramental table.

'Good evening, Father.'

'I'm not your father. If you must address me by any title, it should be Reverend. What are you doing here? And get down from that table. It is where we take the sacrament.'

'I'm just fine right here.'

'Do you respect nothing, young man? I know you are not of our Church but we worship the same God. Do you remember nothing you were taught?'

'When I was a boy the Mass was in Latin so that passed over my poor, ill-educated head. The sermon was in English but I was too worried about getting frostbite in my feet and fingers to be paying the priest any mind. We could have done with a few fires of damnation just to warm the place up a bit.'

'What do you want?'

'Now I've heard about the lesson you gave here this morning. Don't you know better than to be upsetting people like that, you old shitehawk? I think it's time you were given a lesson yourself.'

'This is a house of worship and I its ordained minister. You will leave immediately.'

'I'm not going anywhere until you've learnt your lesson.'

The wrath of righteous anger surged in the Reverend John's breast as he strode through the chapel. The young man sprang down and gripped the minister by the throat, span him round and held him pinioned to the table.

'That's a fine font you have there. Now if I remember rightly its purpose is for the washing away of sin. How about we give it a go?'

He transferred his grip to his victim's collar and dragged him to the font. The young man held the minister's head under the water for a while before pulling him up, gasping and retching.

'Now I'd like to hear you sing. A nice little hymn, perhaps. Maybe one you sang this morning.'

'Please…'

'Sing!'

'Nearer, my God, to Thee, nearer to Thee... e'en though it be a cross that raiseth me...'

Water filled his nose and throat as his head was forced beneath the water again. He could feel his legs growing limp and consciousness begin to fade. Then there was blinding light and burning air but he could breathe.

'Sing. Come on. Put some life into it.'

'Still all my song shall be nearer, my God, to Thee... nearer, my God, to Thee, nearer to Thee.'

Under the water again. This time Reverend John had no inclination to fight against the darkness. Perhaps if he relaxed and welcomed the water into his lungs he would find peace. Peace in the welcoming arms of the Lord our Saviour. After all, this is what had been promised. This is what he rightly deserved.

When the first horror of doubt assailed him, it was too late to fight his way back.

Seán Tyrone tossed the body over his shoulder and left the chapel. There was no one about so he was able to cross Old Bridge Road and enter Drewlys Farm unobserved. In a corner of the field lay a hillock of dung, steaming in the cold night air. A spade stuck up from the pile. Tyrone threw down his burden and began to shovel the stinking ordure over the corpse; in a short while it was covered completely and the heap restored to order. He went back to the chapel and washed his hands in the font before returning to the Deryn Du.

The Moon

Now the moon shines bright over Aberuffern
The crows hop and skip to avoid its light
But there's no escape as they caw and cackle
As the moon lights each black beast
Of Aberuffern

Now the moon shines yellow over Aberuffern
Creatures scuttle and snarl to avoid its light
But there's no way out as they bite each other
As the moon lights each black beast
Of Aberuffern

The Fragile Nature of Innocence

I lay with her one blissful night,
For me the first and sweetest time;
Until day dawned, by candlelight
I sweated out a lovesick rhyme.
That morning when she passed me by,
The hussy would not meet my eye.

Lewis ap Bwgan

Back on Commercial Street I saw a light in the middle of the road. Three ragged people, two men and a woman, sat about an open fire. I walked up unnoticed. As they passed a bottle between them, they cackled at something unspoken. A joke they each knew so well it no longer needed the telling.

'That's a good one,' said the woman.

One of the men wore an eyepatch.

'You're right there,' he said. 'It's a good one isn't it, Dafydd?'

'It's a good one all right.'

The one-eyed man looked up and saw me.

'Who's this then?'

The woman stared at me and spat into the fire. Her phlegm hissed and crackled.

'He's no one.'

'So why's he here?' said the one-eyed man.

'He has nowhere else to be. Isn't that right, Dafydd?'

'I'd say that was about right.'

'So who are you, butt?'

'He's nobody,' said the woman, still holding me with her cold staring eyes.

'But he's here. Would you agree, Dafydd?'

'He's here, certain enough.'

'Then we should welcome him,' said the one-eyed man.

'Tell him to lose himself.'

'No no no, Mair. We have us a new friend here. Let us learn his name and welcome him unto our circle.'

'He's nothing. That's right, Dafydd?'

'I goes along with that.'

The conversation was not going my way. For want of anything better to say, I indicated the patch.

'So… how did you lose the eye?'

'Ah, that's a sad story. It was during the war…'

'Which war?'

'It doesn't matter. That's another story altogether. Anyway, I was anxious not to be called up on account of my various commitments, obligations and ailments.'

'Like your yellow belly,' said Mair.

'Enough, woman. So I went to my Uncle Hywel for advice. He had lost his eye in an incident involving his wife, a pan of boiling water and a local girl he was on friendly terms with and he offered me the lend of his black eyepatch to get over the medical. I turned up to see the doctor and all went as planned so I had a few drinks with the recruiting sergeant by way of celebration. Then I caught the bus and was overcome by a terrible tiredness so I dozed off for a little while. Then I went to my uncle's house to tell him the news and return his property. Here you must steel yourself to learn the awful truth of what had befallen me. When I removed the patch there it was.'

'There was what?'

'Nothing, lad. Where once I had been the proud owner of a matching pair I now had but one eye and one black and dreadful socket. Do you want to see?'

'No thanks. What had happened?'

'Theft, my boy. While I was asleep on the bus, some despicable opportunist had lifted the patch and stolen my eye.'

'That's terrible. Why would they have done that?'

'I have given that very question much thought, lad. My eye would have had very little resale value and although times were hard I don't think the miscreant could have been driven by hunger. I have also considered divine retribution for the harmless deception I had practised, but was loath to credit the vengeful God of the Old Testament with the sense of humour necessary to conceive and perform such an act. Which can only lead me to one conclusion.'

'Which is what?'

'It was stolen for a laugh. A story they could tell their friends in the pub, perhaps even producing the organ for their further amusement. And afterwards the eye would have been tossed over a hedge or thrown to a dog while I am cursed to walk through life thus disfigured.'

'I has not heard so much cachu since the last time you told that story,' said Mair. 'And anyway, it was a cat not a dog.'

'What was that?'

'I said nothing did I, Dafydd?'

'I heard nothing but then I stopped listening some little while ago.'

Mair spat another ball of phlegm into the fire and regarded me generally.

'That's a nice pair of strides he's wearing, Jâms.'

'Straight from the shop wouldn't you say, Dafydd?'

'Probably still have the price sticker on.'

'They'd fit you nicely,' said Mair. 'Come on, butty. Give Dafydd a go of trying them on. Just look at the state of his knackered kecks. Another few days and we'll have to be looking at his fat hairy old arse day and night and we woudn't want that, would we Dafydd?'

'The shame would have my old mother turning in her grave, Mair.'

'So off with them.'

'You're joking sure enough.'

She stood and took a step towards me.

'Does I look like I'm joking? I doesn't even like jokes. I has never even laughed once at a joke in my whole life has I, Dafydd?'

'I has never heard you laugh once in all the years I has known you.'

'You're not having them,' I said, backing away.

'I hates to contradict you but we are. Jâms, Dafydd… grab his arms.'

They were on me in an instant.

'No.'

The two men held me powerless as the woman undid my trousers and pulled them down. I felt the heat of the fire on my legs.

'His underpants smells fresh and clean as well. You could do with a pair of pants, couldn't you Jâms?'

'It is an embarassment to say I have not a pair to my name. The chafing is something wicked.'

'Then we'll have them as well and have a look at what you've got down there. And if it's up to scratch there might be something you has for me as well.'

'His dick's probably clean enough to stir your tea with, eh Dafydd?'

'And eat your biscuits off his arse.'

I struggled to free myself but the effort was useless.

'No. Wait.'

The witch was about to pull down my underpants, but there it was. My father's pistol had appeared in my hand again. The two men dropped their hold on me and stepped back.

'Mair. He's got a bastard pistol.'

'I sees that, twpsyn. And what's more, I do recognise it.'

I moved to where I covered all three of them, and pulled up my trousers with my free hand.

'So do I. How about you, Dafydd?'

'There's no doubt about it, Jâms.'

'Any of you scum take a step and it will be your last.' I could barely recognise my own voice. Mair had not taken her eyes from the pistol.

'It is the pistol of Seán Tyrone,' she said. 'Who are you and where to did you get it?'

'I am the son of Seán Tyrone.'

The ragged people exchanged looks. Mair stepped forward wearing an ingratiating smile. The effect was hideous.

'Now you does understand all that was only a joke.'

'I thought you had no time for jokes.'

'Oh no. I do love a good joke, I does. Dafydd will tell you, won't you Dafydd?

'There is no one for joking like Mair.'

'Jâms?'

'I have lost count of the number of people Mair has had in stitches over the years.'

I silenced them with a wave of the pistol.

'Where can I find my father?'

Mair pushed Jâms forward. He avoided my eye and spoke to the pistol.

'Give that pub over there a go. The Deryn Du. They might be able to help you there.'

'There's nothing we knows,' said the woman, 'is there Dafydd?'

'Nothing at all. Dim byd o gwbl.'

I looked at them steadily.

'The Deryn Du? Is that so? Any one of you try to follow me and you'll be following me to hell.'

'You're there already, butt.'

It was the woman that had spoken. I directed the pistol at her.

'What was that you said?'

'Nothing,' said Jâms. 'She said nothing. Isn't that right Dafydd?'

'I did not hear a word spoken.'

I left the three ragged people to their fire and approached the Deryn Du.

How Mary Met Her Death

Mary had always preferred the company of boys to that of her own sex. As a child she was dismissive of the dolls she was given and any fine clothing that came her way was soon reduced to rags. She did not wish to be a boy herself but was attracted to their pursuits, which among her circle included swearing, fighting, spitting, unwholesome discussion of the baser bodily functions and demonstrating a disdain for all authority both secular and sacred. When she grew older she would occasionally take a boy for a noisy and turbulent ride but her attitude to these brief couplings was there with smoking, drinking, gambling and, of course, fighting.

She had an elder sister whom she visited from time to time. Sarah had married young and now had three children to keep her at home. Mary enjoyed these visits as they gave her the opportunity to observe at first hand the scene of how things might have panned out should she have gone the way of dolls and fine clothing. Sarah saw things differently.

'One day you'll meet someone and everything will change for you. You may pity me now and scorn my home, my husband and my three fine children but one day the wind will change and so will you.'

Mary laughed.

'Then you can say you told me so, but I don't see it myself.'

She took a final look at the unwashed dishes, the tear-stained brats and her sister's sleep-starved face and went down to meet her friends at the club.

Mary was well liked and respected by the regulars of the Inferno. The dancers parted as she walked to the bar. None of the men attempted to approach her; her scorn for dancing was well known and those who had tried to engage her this way would not make the mistake again. A drink was waiting for her as she took her place among her cronies. As was her habit, Mary made a brief assessment of the bar to check that all was as it should be and always had been.

A table at the other side of the club was occupied by three men. Two had their backs to the bar but the man on the far side was a stranger. He was a well-built man with jet-black hair, greased back in waves from his forehead. The stranger held the attention of the other two with a joke or a tale he was telling. When it ended all three laughed and she caught the sudden flash of a gold tooth. The stranger met her eyes as though made electrically aware of her attention. Mary turned her eyes away instantly and joined in the banter with her friends. She avoided looking his way again.

The night passed as had many others with dares and drinks and casual cruelty. Mary and her friends were, as usual, the last to leave and outside the Inferno they made their separate ways home.

Not long after having closed the front door, Mary heard the metal clunk of the letterbox. A slip of paper lay on the doormat. She took it into the light of the bedroom and read:

> Drop by drop, you torture me,
> The rhythm beats incessantly
> Trapped, transfixed; try as I may,
> I cannot turn my eyes away.

She folded the slip of paper and put it in her pocket.

The following day, Mary was sitting in her sister's kitchen when she remembered the note. In truth, it had never been far from her mind. She passed it to Sarah.

'What do you think of this?'

Sarah read, eyebrows raised.

'Well now,' she said. 'It looks like you have an admirer.'

'So you don't think it's a threat?' said Mary. 'Or a warning?'

'Why? Are you afraid?'

Mary scoffed at the idea.

'Trust me,' said her sister. 'Someone's set their cap at you. Any idea who?'

Mary knew none of her acquaintance who would ever dream of such a thing. Thoughtfully, she walked through the village to the Inferno.

At the bar with her friends, she reluctantly found her gaze drawn to the table at the other side of the club. The stranger was there but alone tonight. Again he seemed to sense her eyes upon him and met them with his own. Again Mary turned away and avoided looking in that direction again. She felt anger against this timid self; why was it not demanding explanation of this naked attention, and demanding vengeance for this rude intrusion? He was a well-built man, but she had brought down bigger and had her lads behind her. It was against all reason. When, shortly before closing time, she quickly glanced across the emptying room, the stranger had gone and Mary felt relieved of a weight that had burdened her all evening.

She hesitated before letting herself in and looked down at the doormat. Yes, there was another slip of paper. Mary seized it and read.

> One by one, my friends arise
> They see the madness in my eyes
> It was not there two nights ago
> If I am mad, you made me so.

The next day, Sarah laughed as she handed the note back to her sister.

'He's persistent, this lad of yours. Still no idea who he might be?'

'I have an idea,' said Mary. 'But I'm not at all sure it means what you think it means. This talk of torture and madness. Where are the birds and the flowers and the moon and the stars?'

'Would you have any patience with any man who carried that sort of thing around in his head?'

Mary was again thoughtful as she walked through the village.

Leaning against the bar of the Inferno, she swore to herself that nothing would make her give the most cursory glance across the room to that table. Luckily the club was busy that night and the floor was jammed with dancers; no clear view would have been available even if Mary had weakened.

As the evening drew to a close the dancefloor cleared. Against her will she found her eyes drawn to that forbidden corner. Two lads and two girls she had known since school were sat at the table. The stranger was not there if ever he had been.

At home the doormat was bare. Mary felt a strange sensation that she did not like and quickly shrugged off. She went to the bedroom and began to undress.

Clunk.

She rushed to the door in her barefeet and shift and plucked up the note.

> Step by step, you draw me near
> And I approach, despite my fear
> You have me wholly in your power
> Dark Lady of the Midnight Hour.

Without a thought in her head, Mary opened the door. Across the street stood a well-built man with jet-black hair, greased back in waves from his forehead. He smiled and the gold tooth flashed in the moonlight as he crossed the street.

The next morning, Mary went to her sister's to borrow a dress and a pair of high heels.

At the Inferno, her absence was quickly noted. After a few nights her friends and acquaintances began to show something that could be mistaken for concern. It was even suggested someone might call at her flat, but there was no volunteer. Respect for Mary contained no small element of unmanly fear. The fact was they had all passed Mary in the village, but so changed was she in appearance and manner they had failed to recognise her. She in turn had not called out or acknowledged them in any way; her eyes were fixed only on the well-built man with jet-black hair whose arm she held with such pride.

Mary continued to visit her sister from time to time. Of course, Sarah was delighted with the turn of events.

'I told you the wind would change,' she said. 'Has he said anything yet?'

'Said anything about what?'

'You know. Settling down. Getting married and starting a family, that sort of thing. You've gone red. Who would've ever thought I'd see my little sister blush?'

Mary denied it, but was lost in thought as she walked through the village. By the time she reached home, she had made a decision. Although there was no doubt she had undergone a metamorphosis little short of a miracle, she had retained the forward and forthright edge of her nature. She took her lover by the hands and looked into his eyes.

'We must talk about the future.'

'The future?' he said. 'Well… no doubt there'll be jet-packs and trips to Mars and the like…'

'No. Our future. Have you never thought that we might get married and maybe start a family? Has the thought never occurred to you?'

He stared at her for a moment and then smiled his gold-toothed smile. Slowly he began to laugh, a laugh that welled up from his belly.

'Don't,' said Mary. 'Don't laugh at me, I'm serious.'

'Marry? Marry you? Sweetheart, I don't even like you.'

'But the poems,' said Mary. 'Those notes you put through my door. I've kept them with me always.'

'They weren't mine. I copied them from a book in the library. I only bothered with them for the amusement of having a hard-faced bitch like you dancing girlish attention on me. Marriage? That's a corker. Why should I want to saddle myself with a raddled old tart like you?'

Mary sat on the bed and heard the front door slam shut. For a time she was coldly empty but then she began to feel the embers of a fire begin to glow in the depths of her guts. The flames began to flicker, kindled by a molten mass of lava that surged upward filling every part of her until erupting in an almost unending scream that could only have originated in the bowels of Hell itself.

And then silence. She looked down at the dress she was wearing; it was torn and the flesh beneath was riven with scratches. Fresh blood stained her fingers. A fly buzzed angrily about the room and she watched it with dull eyes. Someone banged on the front door and then went away. Gradually the everyday sounds of the world amassed to fill the silence and life went on like an insult. Let it never be said that Mary would let an insult go unavenged.

Sarah had a spare key to the flat. She buried her sister in a fine silk dress and a coronet of fresh white flowers.

The Girl in the Deryn Du

The new settlement, which had hitherto been known as Parrytown (after the Parry Glamorgan Colliery Company), found itself in need of an officially recognised name. To this end, a committee formed of members of the Parish Council and representatives of the area's commercial interests crowded into the Deryn Du public house on January 17, 1895. After much heated debate and the abandonment of many fanciful suggestions, the name 'Aberuffern' was proposed and seconded. As to the identity of the proposer and the explanation of the Committee's unanimous acceptance of his proposal, these matters are lost to history; unfortunately the Secretary fell victim to a sudden malady and had to be escorted to his home, thus leaving this portion of the proceedings unminuted. When interviewed in later years, the surviving committee members had but little recollection of events, so the naming of Aberuffern must remain a matter for conjecture only.

Huntley, *op. cit.*

I walked into the Deryn Du and there behind the bar was the most beautiful and ephemeral girl I'd ever seen. She smiled at me. It was like she'd been stolen by the fairy folk and abandoned when they weren't believed in any more. But, for a few wordless moments, I believed. Then she spoke.

'I'm sorry love, we're closed now. Been closed for some time.'

'I don't want a drink. I want to talk to you.'

'Talk to me, cariad? There's a novelty. Talk to me about what exactly?'

'My father.'

'What was it, child abuse? Did he just beat you or was there other things? Take a stool, my lovely. There's a drink I can find you from somewhere. You tell me all about it. When did it start, when you were a dwt? That's the way it usually is.'

'No, you don't understand. There was nothing like that. I hardly knew the man.'

'Oh I understand all right. There's an awful lot of it goes on... we had some whisky here once. No, it's gone. Vodka? No, this one's dry as a bone.'

'It doesn't matter,' I said, feeling a desperate need to look into her eyes again.

'You go on telling me about what your dad did to you… there was creme de menthe but I had to chuck it out. Gone crystallised in the bottle and you wouldn't have liked it anyway.'

'I don't want a drink.'

'I expect he had an unhappy childhood himself and took it out on you… what do you think it says on this bottle here? Can't make it out myself what with the dust on the label.'

'Napoleon Brandy Style Distillate. Produce of Albania.'

'At least there's some of that left. I'll pour you a glass.'

'Thanks. But I don't have any money.'

'This one's on the house, my poor love. I might have one myself and join you your side of the bar.'

She opened the counter hatch and came round to sit on the stool next to mine. I felt the warmth infuse my body through her thin white dress. She smelled like a forest in summer.

'You have no shoes on your feet,' I said.

'This stuff tastes like murder, doesn't it? Still, it's all there is. What's your name, cariad?'

'Jack. What's yours?'

'They call me Peri.'

'Peri. It's a pretty name.'

'Move your stool closer, Jack. What time is it?'

I looked at my watch.

'Almost midnight. Why?'

'I must bolt the door.'

She leapt up, overturning her stool in her haste, hurried to the door and rammed the heavy bolt home.

'What is it? Are you expecting anyone? Surely not customers, at this time of night.'

She shook her head.

'Then who?'

'The Mari Lwyd.' Seeing my look of blank incomprehension, she elaborated.

'They used to come round at Christmas with a horse's skull wearing a white sheet like a shroud. That all died out when my granddad was only a boy. But now... now they comes round every night, twelve on the dot and I don't dare let them in.'

She was interrupted by a violent pounding on the door.

Several voices began to sing discordantly –

> Wel dyma n'in diwad
> Gyfeillion diniwad
> I ofyn cawn gennad
> I ofyn cawn gennad
> I ofyn cawn gennad i ganu

Peri clutched at my sleeve, her eyes wide with fear.

'What does that mean?' I said.

'They say they're harmless and all they want to is come in and sing to us.'

I shouted at the unseen horde.

'Go away. We've called time already.'

'No,' said Peri. 'You have to sing back to them or they won't listen.'

'Sing what?'

'You have to make it up.'

'But I can't speak a word of Welsh.' (I could not then and cannot now but have since discovered the lyric to their hideous air.)

'Then sing in English.'

There came another furious pounding at the door. I cleared my throat and, imitating the melody as best I could, extemporised –

We cannot let you in
We've bolted up the door
And your singing's very poor
We've bolted up
We've bolted up
We've bolted up the door

'What now?' I said, but before she could reply the racket started up again –

Mae Mari Lwyd lawen
Y dod yn y dafarn
I ofyn am arian
I ofyn am arian
I ofyn am arian a chwrw

I turned to the girl for a translation.

'They say they're happy to come to the pub to ask for money and beer.'

Taking a deep breath, I sang with all the authority I could muster –

We do not want you here
We've no money or beer
We do not want
We do not want
We do not want you here

There was no immediate reponse from outside. Then a sepulchral voice muttered something in Welsh. A long silence followed during which we hardly dared breathe. Then the girl turned to me and beamed.

'That was brilliant, Jack. They won't be coming back, not tonight anyway. Now where were we? Oh that's right, you were telling me all about your dad.'

'My dad? Yes, my dad. You might know him. His name is Seán Tyrone.'

She looked away. I wanted to kiss her ear.

'Is there some more in that bottle?' she said and poured herself another full glass which she emptied in one draught.

'I think I love you,' I said. First she showed no reaction; it occurred to me that perhaps I had not voiced my thought. But then she answered, her face still turned from mine.

'Oh no, you don't want to do that.'

'Why?'

'I can't be touched. Not by you. But if you wants to look for your dad, go to the Aberuffern pit. It's closed down now but there's some there who'll tell you what you need to know. Hwyl dda, bach.'

'And then can I come back here?'

She turned to me and smiled.

'It's probably best if you don't, cariad.'

I left the Deryn Du with fire in my stomach and love in my heart.

Lord of the Manor

He had no liking for work
He'd take no orders from the boss
Down the shaft he fell
Now Seán became the owner of the pit.

The Ballad of Seán Tyrone

Arthur Bryn Parry poked gloomily at an unsympathetic rasher of bacon on his plate. He felt he had much to feel gloomy about that morning and the seeming infinity of mornings that stretched before him into an uncertain future. The fortune amassed by his fathers with such daring and alacrity had dwindled under his stewardship to a net income barely capable of sustaining the business and this house, built by his grandfather in more prosperous times. The Coal Board had passed over the Parry Glamorgan Colliery

Company for nationalisation and since then he had been forced to sell off the other businesses in order to feed the ever gaping maw of Aberuffern pit. The small consolation was that no heir existed to bother him with frustrated expectations; his wife had been a pale and sickly creature who had failed to survive the trauma of marriage and bear him any sons. He was the last of his line and would in all probability take the family name to a pauper's grave. Mr Parry pushed the uneaten food away with a deep sigh of morbid resignation.

The brass bell behind the front door tolled and he heard the maid prosecute a muffled exchange with the caller. She came into the breakfast room.

'There's a man to see you. A Mister O'Brien.'

'O'Brien? On what business?'

'He wouldn't say. I told him you were having your breakfast but he wouldn't be put off.'

'Very well, Margaret. Show him into the office and ask him to wait.'

'All right, and then I'll be off to the shops if that's convenient. Is there anything I can get you?'

He shook his head as though tormented by a wasp. O'Brien. The name was unfamiliar. A creditor or his dun in all likelihood. Wearily, Mr Parry rose to his feet, automatically wiping his lips on the napkin although no food had passed that way. He might as well see this man despite having nothing to give or promise him.

The man stood up as Parry entered the room. He was a youngish-looking fellow, though grey hairs had begun to advance through the jet-black hair and premature lines of dissipation creased the blue-white skin at the eyes, forehead and mouth.

'Mr O'Brien? I don't believe I've had the pleasure. How can I help you? Please be seated.'

'Thank you, sir. It's Seán O'Brien. I work the nine foot seam at Aberuffern pit.'

Mr Parry raised his eyebrows, inviting the man to continue.

'I've been there some years, sir, and I got to thinking that what with Jones having that accident…'

'Jones?' said Mr Parry. 'Which Jones? I employ so many.'

'Lazarus Jones. It doesn't look as though he'll be coming back this time which means there's an opening for a foreman on my shift.'

'And you think you're the man to fill it.'

'Yes, sir.'

Mr Parry leaned back in his chair and idly fingered an ornament on the desk. It was a moment before he recognised it as the medal, now mounted on a block of polished wood, he had won as a boy for performance in the backstroke. The one unassailable achievement of his otherwise moribund existence.

'Sir?'

'Foreman, you say. You'd like to be preferred for the position of foreman in my pit. Tell me, O'Brien. Are you an ambitious man? No, don't answer. I can see that you are. The only criticism I have regards the level you strive to attain. You are still young, strong and confident enough to beard me in my lair, but for what prize? The duties of a foreman are scarcely less onerous than those you hold already and, I assume, only marginally better rewarded. Aim higher, O'Brien. Ask and you shall receive and what is not given freely must be taken. Answer me this, O'Brien. Would you like to find yourself in my position?'

'One day perhaps, sir.'

'Then you are every inch the rogue and scoundrel I took you for. You shall have what you desire. Not some day but this day – this very instant.'

Mr O'Brien opened a drawer and took out a sheaf of papers. Taking a pen, he began to write.

'Here are the deeds to this house, now transferred to one Seán O'Brien.'

He pushed the document across the desk.

'And here are the papers concerning ownership of the Parry Glamorgan Colliery Company, made over to the same.'

The man held the papers, shaking his head in bewilderment.

'I don't understand,' he said. 'This can't be right. Besides, aren't there some legalities to be observed?'

'I wouldn't have thought that would bother your conscience even should you possess such a useless irrelevance. I'm sure you can prevail on some blackguard of your acquaintance to state he was witness to my signature. Take it all, O'Brien. And may it bring you as much happiness as it has me.'

Mr Parry rose and strode to the front door, barely pausing to take his hat from the stand. The man followed, still clutching the deeds.

'What is it? Oh I do apologise, my good fellow. Here are the keys. And you have a maid. Her name is

Margaret and she dislikes any diminutive form. Treat her kindly.'

Mr Parry continued his walk through the grounds and down the valley to the village. In Commercial Street people stood to one side as he passed and he acknowledged their respectful subservience with a cheery nod. He did not break his step until he reached the riverbank. Here he removed his jacket, unlaced his shoes and took off his hat. Mr Parry stepped into the rapidly moving current and waded out to a depth which allowed him to float on his back where, after taking a few moments to accustom himself to the long unfamiliar sensation, he relaxed and let the river carry him where it would. He closed his eyes and anticipated the journey. He would be borne to where the river joined the Taff which would eventually take him through the city, disgorging his body into the Bristol Channel and finally the epic expanses of the Atlantic Ocean. Mr Parry smiled in contentment.

Back at the Manor House, the man found himself in the breakfast room. He relieved himself of the pistol tucked into his waistband before sitting down to finish Mr Parry's breakfast.

The Clouds

The clouds above the Aberuffern pit
Took aspect of faces
Looking down at Jack

We know you
You are the son of Seán Tyrone
We know your flesh and recognise your bone
For you are the son of Seán Tyrone

The clouds climbed down and grinned at Jack
Took the spaces
Surrounding him

We see you
You are the son of Seán Tyrone
We know your flesh and recognise your bone
For you are the son of Seán Tyrone
And the clouds dispersed
Vapour in the sky
Faces gone
Goodbye, goodbye

The Sins of the Father

My father was a good man;
Upright and sober, neat and trim.
He beat me for my failings,
But I could find no fault in him.

Now I am old and fading
I sag and creak, I carp and frown
Thank God I have no children
To say their father let them down.

Lewis ap Bwgan

Two men and a woman sat by the shaft. One of the men held a crutch and I could see that his left trouser leg hung empty from the knee. I approached them and the woman looked up sharply.

'Who the hell are you?'

'He certainly looks familiar,' said the one-legged man. 'Wouldn't you say so, Dewi?'

'To my eye at least.'

'I'm Jack O'Brien. I'm the son of the man you know here as Seán Tyrone.'

'So you are his son?' said the one-legged man.

'I am.'

The woman spat into the coal dust.

'Let's put him down the shaft, Jimmy.'

'Not yet. Let's hear what he has to say, eh Dewi?'

'A word or two might be of interest.'

'He's a good-looking lad,' said Jimmy.

'So was his father and see what he did,' said the woman.

'Let's not jump to any hasty judgments, Maria. We'll talk to the lad. That's the best way to proceed isn't it, Dewi?'

'I would proceed no further.'

'Down the lift shaft.'

'Not yet, Maria. We should tell the boy about his father. Wouldn't you agree, Dewi?'

'It would be just about fair, I'd say.'

'Why bother?' said Maria.

'Because bothering about these things is what makes us human beings and our humanity is all we have to cling to, isn't it?'

'I couldn't be arsed,' said Maria. 'What about you, Dewi?'

'Perhaps given the right climate and circumstance I could be arsed.'

'Down the shaft with him.'

I felt uncomfortable, so ventured a change of subject.

'So how did you lose the leg?'

'An ingrowing toenail, my boy.'

'An ingrowing toenail? I've never heard of anyone losing their leg due to one of those.'

'It is a story that will sadden your heart and open your eyes to the injustice of life. Do you still wish to hear it?'

'I do.'

'My big toe had been causing me no little discomfort for some time so I took it to the doctor. He had one look at it and made an instant diagnosis. I had an ingrowing nail. It would necessitate a visit to the hospital but he assured me the operation was a simple one and I would be back to rights in no time at all.

‘So I took myself off to the hospital where I was admitted to a small surgical ward and put to bed.

‘There was only one other patient on my ward – a cheery old soul whose leg had been crushed beyond repair in a fall at this very pit. He was called Lazarus Jones; not his birthname you understand but a nickname he had won for being written off as dead many times only to effect a miraculous resurrection on each occasion. The time passed pleasantly as I listened to him relate his gory and horrific experiences and presently we were both put under in preparation for our respective operations.

‘I have no idea how much time had passed before I regained consciousness but the first thing I was aware of was Lazarus Jones sitting on the foot of my bed, grinning cheerfully. Weakly, I asked him how his operation had gone. Remarkably well he said, showing me his leg. The foot was bare save from some bandaging to his big toe. I expressed my surprise as we had both expected the leg to be amputated at the knee, such was the extent and severity of his injury. He shrugged, bade me farewell and limped homeward.

'It was now that I became aware of a terrible pain in my left leg. I lifted the blanket and there it was.'

'There was what?'

He paused, leaving me in great suspense.

'Nothing. The leg had gone, disappeared, vanished into the ether. It was immediately obvious what had happened. Lazarus Jones had been operated on for my ingrowing toenail and my leg had been amputated in place of his.'

'But that's terrrible. Couldn't they have sewn it back on once the mistake was discovered?'

'Perhaps. But the missing limb had been sent to the anatomical department for dissection. Some medical students had appropriated the leg and taken it to a party with the drunken intention of using it to frighten some young nurses. In the course of the evening it was subjected to various indignities and was in no state for reattachment to be considered when it was eventually returned to the hospital. There is however one good thing to have come from the whole sorry incident. I found a man whose right leg is missing and came to an arrangement whereby we share a pair of shoes between us. This has represented a considerable saving on the cost of footwear over the years.'

'Pull the other one,' said Maria.

'It's easy for you to say that,' said Jimmy. 'If only I could. Now. A word or two about the man you say is your father. Seán Tyrone.'

He hopped forward and cleared his throat.

He came here from over the water
And he banged up the landlord's daughter
The landlord of the Deryn Du
Haunted now by the landlord's daughter
With the memory of her father's slaughter
Hanged in the backroom of the Deryn Du
By the man who crossed from over the water
Banged up the daughter of the Deryn Du
Whose father wouldn't have him
As a member of the family.

And from the depths of his demon-ridden mind
Came the thought of murder
Couldn't be turned away
So he took his knife
And his pistol in his hand
A rope across his shoulders
And he hanged a man.

Jimmy bowed and the other two applauded.

'But that was only the beginning of his bastard sins wasn't it, Dewi?' said Maria.

'Only the beginning.'

'Have you tried to buy a drink in the Deryn Du?' said Jimmy. 'It's as dry as the old landlord's bones.'

'And what has that to do with my father?'

'He claimed ownership of the place.'

'Have you seen the graveyard and wondered why there's no minister to keep it in order?' said Maria.

'So what? There's no priest.'

'Seán Tyrone saw to that.'

'Or considered why this pit might have gone to rack and ruin?'

'How is that my father's fault?'

'He starved it of money and men.'

'Or found it strange that even the police won't come near the place?' said Maria.

'It's lies. A pack of lies.'

'I'm sorry, my boy. Every word of it is true. Isn't that so, Dewi?'

'The gospel truth.'

'And it's all down to your bastard father.'

'No.'

'Maria's right. Your father is to blame for the death of Aberuffern.'

'You're liars. All liars.'

'You have to face up to it, boy. Your father, Seán Tyrone, was probably the most evil man to walk this Earth.'

'No.'

A terrible rage overwhelmed me and took control of my actions. I grasped the one-legged man by the throat and shook him like a dog would a rat. The woman pummelled my back and kicked at my legs, screeching like a harpie.

'Let him go. Dewi, do something.'

The other man bit at my fingers in an attempt to release my grip on his friend's windpipe and the woman redoubled her efforts but I was oblivious to their violence. All I desired was this man's death and all my determination was to that end. His body limpened in my hold and his empty trouser leg waved in pathetic surrender.

Then I was aware of the woman's hand in my jacket pocket. The pistol was in her hand and she held it to my head.

'Now will you let go?'

I let go and Jimmy fell to the ground.

'My God. What have I done?'

'You've proved yourself to be the son of Seán Tyrone, that's what you've done. Now I'm going to finish you with your father's own pistol.'

Jimmy raised himself up on one hand and rubbed his neck with the other.

'No, Maria. He's done me no real harm.'

'Then down the shaft with him. Let him rot with his old man.'

'Let him go. He suffers enough as the son of Seán Tyrone. Wouldn't you agree, Dewi?'

'I'd go along with you that far.'

'Chuck him down the shaft.'

'The lift still works. I can recommend it as a far more comfortable means of transport than the one Maria suggests.'

'My way was good enough for his father. Why shouldn't it be good enough for him?'

'Come now, Maria,' said Jimmy. 'We don't want to incriminate ourselves, do we? As the late Reverend John was fond of quoting, let the dead bury their dead. Don't you agree, Dewi?'

'I almost certainly would if I knew what it meant.'

'Take the lift, my boy. Find your father and go in peace.'

How James Met His Death

When James first opened his eyes on the world three women smiled down on him: his mother, his grandmother and the midwife.

'Look at those bright blue eyes,' said his mother. 'Whoever did they come from? Not me or his father, that's for sure.'

'The girls will be at him like flies on a turd,' said his grandmother.

'He'll be a devil with the ladies,' said the midwife. 'No doubt about that.'

And they were right. When James grew and stopped thinking of girls as a gaggle of nuisances to be abided and no more, he came to appreciate their soft hair, soft hands and soft lips. But more than these, it was the softening of their eyes when they first met his, the melting away of resistance, that drew James to women.

James' parents were successful in a small way of business and took pride in seeing their son leave the house each morning in the newest and smartest of fashions their money could buy, walking through the village with a girl on each arm; everyone seduced by the flash of those bright blue eyes and their promise of perpetual spring.

One day his grandfather asked him how long he intended leading this carefree life. When did he intend taking a wife and making his mark in the world? James replied as though addressing a backward child.

'You are old, Grandfather. You've been old for as long as I've known you. But I am young and have plenty of time to settle down and make my mark in the world, as you put it.'

'You're already going a bit thin on top,' said his grandfather.

'Nothing a little art with the comb won't put right,' said James. 'And I can always wear a hat.'

'A hat? In bed?'

'Should that eventuality arise, I shall turn off the light.'

So James carried on as he always had, but now more often than not with only the one girl on his arm and a hat on his head. But he still had his charm and the semblance of youth and of course, those bright blue eyes.

One day his father took him aside and voiced his concern at James' feckless ways; surely the time had come to look to the future and make some use of his life. James chuckled and replied with a patronising note in his voice.

'You are old, Father. You have been old for as long as I've known you. But I am younger than you and the future is still a distant prospect.'

'You don't smile as you did,' said his father. 'Is there some trouble with your teeth?'

'There are miracles done in the dentist's chair these days, Father.'

'If it's not left for too long.'

'There's always tomorrow to consider such things,' said James, adjusting his hat in the mirror as he left.

Time passed and James buried his grandfather, his father and his mother in succession. He had made no mark in the world nor made any use of his life, but this was of no concern to James. With the benefit of a few drinks, he could approach the mirror without fear. The gouged lines on his forehead, the creased eyelids and crowsfeet, the broken capillaries that embroidered his nose and cheeks with purple, the lizardskin flap that joined his chin to his throat – all these were invisible to James in the dimly lit and fogged glass.

One evening in autumn, James walked through the village and over the bridge to a club that was there. He had not arranged to meet any of the women of his acquaintance, but felt sure that his luck, charm and bright blue eyes would not find him without company that night. He paused at the entrance to recover his breath a little before going in.

The music was louder, surely louder than usual. James bought a drink at the bar and asked the girl next to him what she'd be having. The girl couldn't hear him through the noise so he mimed the offer as best he could. The girl laughed and patted his cheek as one would an elderly and inebriate relative at a wedding. She took two drinks from the barmaid (which she paid for herself) and went to join her friend at a table. Pride and the fear of further humiliation prevented James from following.

In the men's room, James checked his appearance in the mirror. His hat was in place and he had remembered to clean the false teeth, but the light was cruel in this white-tiled room and he turned away from the glass. Perhaps he was coming down with something. Perhaps he should go home and sweat it out. A young man blocked his way.

'All right, Grandpa?' said the young man. 'Isn't this a bit late for you to be out and about? You should be in bed with your Horlicks.'

James ignored him and left the men's room. Holding his hat to his head, he pushed his way through the jostling dancers and out on to the street.

It had been raining and James could feel the damp in his bones. He wasn't well. Home, that was the best thing. Home and bed, and tomorrow everything would be all right again. Tomorrow and all the tomorrows that stretched out into that bright and distant future. He pulled up his collar, sank his hands into the depths of his pockets and looked forward to the bed and the bottle that awaited him.

As he walked he became aware of footsteps behind him; more than one person, perhaps three. He knew that to turn his head would be to invite trouble but increased his pace. The footsteps kept tempo with him.

His breath strained at his ribs but he laboured to keep this from his followers; one show of weakness and they would pounce.

'Now, Grandpa,' came the voice. 'Do you have a light?'

There was no point in running; they would be upon him in no time. There was no one to call on for help or to stand witness. There was nothing to do but stand and turn.

Three young hooligans, two lads and a girl. James said nothing but held out his lighter and snapped up a flame. The lad who had spoken cupped one hand round the flame and steadied James' wrist with the other.

'Where's your cigarette?' said James. 'You don't have a cigarette.'

'That's observant of you, Grandpa,' said the lad. He turned to the other hooligan. 'Wouldn't you say so?'

'For an old coot. Observant, I'd say.'

The girl blew out the flame.

'Nice hat, Grandpa,' she said. 'Let's give it a try. Look, he's as bald as a babby's arse.'

'Please. Give it back,' said James, trying to keep his voice steady. 'What do you want? I've got a fiver and a few coppers. Not much, but you're welcome to it.'

The girl spat on the ground.

'We don't want your stinking money. How do we know where it's been? Probably stuffed up your scrawny old arse for safekeeping.'

'I don't want any trouble. Please let go of my wrist.'

The first lad released his hold and began to laugh. The other two joined him as they pushed and span James between them. One fetched a blow on his back that made the false teeth fly from his mouth, which action fuelled their derision to greater heights until James collapsed in a pile at their feet. With their boots they rolled him into the ditch at the side of the road and went on their way.

James lay there, his limbs twitching perhaps in an effort to draw himself up or perhaps convulsing independent of will. Either way the mud sucked him in, filling his nostrils, mouth and lungs and dimming those bright blue eyes. Which is how they found him in the morning.

Anghenfil

The Parry family of Cardiff formed the Parry Glamorgan Colliery Company for the sole purpose of sinking the pit at Aberuffern. Their fortune had already been established through various commercial concerns dating back to before the Slavery Abolition Act of 1833 which possibly explains the soubriquet given the *pater familias*: 'Bryn the Blackbirder'. It should be noted here that this appellation is unconnected with that of the Deryn Du (black bird) public house. An inn of that name has stood on the site since the seventeenth century, possibly earlier, although the house itself has been modified several times in the intervening years and retains little of what must have been its original character. It may be interesting to observe that the inn sign (date and artist unknown) appears to depict a crow, for which the more usual Welsh would be *brân*.

Huntley, *op.cit.*

I wanted to see Peri again before I went down the shaft; perhaps it was an act of procrastination, fear of what spirits might lurk in that dark and dreadful place. Looking back I cannot say.

I left the people at the Aberuffern colliery and returned to the Deryn Du. The door was ajar and I walked in. Peri wasn't there so I sat on a stool and waited. Moments later I heard a voice sobbing in a room above. I went to the foot of the stair.

'Peri? It's me. Jack. Jack O'Brien, son of Seán Tyrone.'

She called down to me.

'Go now. I don't want to see you or you to see me.'

I climbed the stair. A door stood open but the room was in darkness.

'Turn on the light. What don't you want me to see?'

She hesitated before answering.

'Wait. I will light a candle.'

I could not stop myself from crying out.

'My God. What is that?'

In her soft white arms she held a creature of pain wrapped in rags, writhing and turning, angles suggesting limbs jutting out like a broken concertina, wheezing and mewling in torment.

'Now here, here is your sister.'

'My sister?'

'Yes, Jack O'Brien son of Seán Tyrone. You may think her a monster but she is my daughter. Her flesh is my flesh and her spirit is my spirit. And Jack – her blood is the blood that also runs through your veins, the blood of that cursed man.

'Look at your sister, Jack. She's not so pretty as you, is she? Do you want to hold her?'

'No.'

'Hold her. Her name is Anghenfil. Not a pretty name but then neither is she. Take your sister in your arms. Feel the warmth of the life your father brought into the world.'

She held out the child but I stepped back to the head of the staircase and gripped the rail. Suddenly came the sound of a terrible commotion from the bar. Tables were being turned over, chairs broken, glasses smashed. I drew my pistol and prepared to face the intruders.

'Stop. Don't go down there.'

'But I must. They're tearing the place apart.'

'Stay where you are and put away your father's pistol. There's no one there.'

Had she lost her reason? Certainly there were no voices to be heard raised in the lust of carnage or coarse laughter as they went about their work of wilful vandalism. But even so their presence was obvious and evident in that cacophony of demolition and destruction.

'Can't you hear them? If I don't stop them there'll be nothing left to wreck and then they'll be up here and at us.'

'I said there's no one there.'

'Then I am truly mad if I cannot trust what my own ears tell me so clearly.'

Then the child screeched. It was a sound that filled my head and almost distracted me from the chaos downstairs. The screeching continued in short rhythmic bursts each louder and more piercing than the last.

'Jesus. Please make her stop. Can't you make her stop?'

'Why would I stop her? She's laughing and she doesn't often laugh. She's laughing at you, Jack.'

Gradually the screeching subsided until there was only racked breathing punctuated by irregular gasps of pain. Downstairs all was quiet. I went down and saw the wreckage. There was not a soul in the place and the door was closed as I had left it.

'They're gone. Thank God they're gone.'

'I told you. There was never anyone here.'

'Look at the place. Look at what they've done. How can you say no one's responsible for this?'

'I didn't say no one is responsible. I knows who has done this.'

'Who?'

'Your sister, Jack.'

My mouth gaped.

'Then we are both mad.'

'No. You will find it hard to understand but you must try. My daughter may appear weak and failing in your eyes, but that is because you can't see beyond the flesh. Her spirit is strong and tireless; stronger than yours and mine, much stronger. And from time to time her spirit grows angry at being fettered in the chains and shackles of the flesh and it must break free of its constraints. That is what you heard and what you see here are the consequences. Do you understand?'

'No, but I will try. You say she is my sister.'

'Her father is your father.'

'How? Tell me what happened.'

'My father was the landlord of the Deryn Du. Seán Tyrone was here every evening and it was plain for all to see that he was not here for drink or comradeship but to steal my heart. I was young and knew nothing of men and your father was charming and handsome and in those days he knew how to make me laugh. I can't say I has done much laughing since, cariad.

'He was not a patient man. Once he had set his mind on having something before long it would be his, if not given freely then snatched away. One day he came here to ask my father for his approval of our marriage. When my father refused, Seán Tyrone murdered him.'

'Was it proved? I have heard my father's name slandered by others but seen no evidence to support these accusations.'

'His name? That's almost funny. Let me tell you something, cariad. Not only did Seán Tyrone murder him but he did so in such a terrible way that my father's good name was damned for a sin he did not commit. As for proof, I need none. That night when he came to my bed, to steal not my heart but my innocence, he told me what he had done. Not to beg my forgiveness but to laugh and jeer at me. After he had mocked my father with a string of foul and obscene names, he turned on me. And when the words stopped the fists began.

'I was not always the wreck of a human being you see here, Jack. It was not only your father's fists and boots pounding my body day after day, week after week, year after year that destroyed me. It was the spiteful, malicious and brutal tongue whose lash I dreaded most. There was no shrinking from that scourge and the weals still weep. Given time the flesh may heal but a spirit once broken carries its pain forever. He was an awful shit, your father. You may find it hard to believe it now, Jack, but once people did call me beautiful.'

Tears sparkled in her eyes. She wiped them away with a golden strand of hair. I felt that if I did not turn my eyes from her glory I would be blinded forever, but I could not.

'You are beautiful, Peri. You are the most beautiful and wondrous creature any mortal could ever believe existed. Peri, I love you. I want you more than anything in the world. Come with me. We'll leave this terrible place, this charnel pit of death and dying.'

'Aberuffern is not a place of death and dying, cariad. It is dead already. Your sister is the only flame of life that burns here and it is my destiny to nurture that flame and ensure that it is never extinguished. That is why I can't go with you.'

'Please.'

'Oh, my poor little love. It's not possible.'

'Why? Why not?'

'I hope you will always remember me with love in your heart. God bless you and keep you, cariad.'

I left the Deryn Du and returned to the pit.

The Detective and His Men

Six coppers came around one night
To try and lock up Seán Tyrone.
Out his pistol came
The six of them were never seen again.

The Ballad of Seán Tyrone

Detective Sergeant Paul Carew pulled off the dual carriageway and drove the mile or two down to Aberuffern. In the station car park he sat with DC Crowther, waiting for the other car to catch up.

'Been here before, Crowther?'

'You're joking,' said Crowther. 'Why would I want to do that? Nothing happens in places like this.'

'You're wrong there, son,' said Carew. 'You're new on this patch, so best you keep an open mind. If you'd been at the briefing on time this morning you'd know a thing or two about Aberuffern.'

'Someone said something about two plods going missing.'

'Kendrick and Morris. Not the sharpest tools in the box, but good to have on your side in a ruck. Last night we had a call-out to the local pub. Run of the mill stuff – a domestic. The barmaid was being knocked about by her ex and one of the customers slipped out to give us a bell.'

'Couldn't the local police have handled it?'

'What local police? Cuts. You used to have a good old-fashioned village bobby sitting on his arse wearing slippers, drinking tea and doing the pools but that was years ago. Tremorgan covers the whole area now.'

'So what happened last night?'

'That's what we're here to find out, son. They didn't radio in but that means nothing. The signal can get dodgy in these parts. The alarm bells started ringing when they didn't report back at the nick. We rang their homes but their wives hadn't heard a peep from them and still hadn't when we called again this morning. That's the set-up so let's get the job done. Where's the Dynamic Duo?'

A squad car pulled into the car park and two uniformed officers came over to join Carew and Crowther.

'Get caught short, did you?' said Carew.

'Stuck behind a lorry, sir,' said the larger of the pair.

'All right, I didn't ask for your life story.'

'So what's the plan?' said the other man.

'Me and Crowther will check out the pub. I want you and Fat Edwards to ask around, see what you can find out from the locals. The usual places – shops, the pit, the chapel and there's a club somewhere just over the river. Oh and there's a farm, they might know something there. Shouldn't take long; you could walk from one end of the place to the other in ten minutes, and that's if you're a tortoise on a zimmer frame. Off you go. Rendezvous at the pub two o'clock – plenty of time to buy me a pint and read me the news.'

Crowther watched them leave.

'Why do you call him Fat Edwards? Doesn't he mind?'

'We call him Fat Edwards because he's a fat bastard and they're both called Edwards.'

'So what do you call the other one?'

'Bald Edwards. No relation. Let's find this pub.'

As they walked into the unlit bar the first thing that struck them was the stillness and quiet. The second, almost instantaneously and with greater force, was the stench of the place. Stale tobacco, stale beer, stale sweat. The carpet stuck to the soles of their shoes and motes of dust floated in the sunlight that shone cruelly through the unwashed panes, illuminating each stain, each derelict web, each peeling wall. The place appeared deserted until a hacking cough alerted them to the presence of an old man sitting at a table in the corner, hawking phlegm into a crumpled tissue.

'Afternoon, lads.'

'Afternoon,' said Carew. 'Who's behind the bar?'

'She's out the back. Tap on one of the pumps.'

Carew took a coin from his pocket and gave a brass handle three brisk raps. A woman answered. A young woman, he thought.

'I'll be with you now.'

The two policemen waited silently. A minute passed. Two. Carew rapped on the brass again.

'I said I'll be there now.'

The woman came out from a door behind the counter, wiping her hands on a bar towel.

'Jesus,' said Crowther.

Carew was not impressed either. The woman was not young as he had thought, but neither was it possible to guess her age. Dirty blonde hair hung in rat-tails around bruised shoulders. The dress had probably been white when new but now showed a greyish hue, patterned with beer and food stains and what to the forensic eye were certainly traces of dried blood. The eyes were red and puffy and the skin was blotched; a vivid contusion marked the left cheek and when she spoke the teeth were chipped and yellow.

'What can I get you?'

'Police,' said Carew, showing his warrant card. 'We were called out to a disturbance reported here last night. Can you tell us anything about it?'

A tortured cry sounded from somewhere in the house.

'What the hell was that?' said Crowther.

'A cat,' said the woman.

'That was no cat.'

'All right. It's my daughter.'

'Hadn't you better check on her?'

'She'll be fine. Now what were you saying? A disturbance? Last night? There was no disturbance last night, was there Kenneth?'

'Quiet as the grave,' said the old man.

'See? I don't know what you're on about. There was no cowing disturbance here last night, not in my pub.'

'Is that right, Grandpa?' said Carew.

'No disturbance here, lads. Quiet as the grave it was.'

'So you didn't see two policemen in here? Two uniformed officers, about ten o'clock it would have been.'

'Police?' said the woman. 'There were no police come last night. He'll tell you, he was here.'

'She's telling you the truth, no word of a lie. There were no coppers in here last night. I would have noticed.'

'You're sure about this, are you?' said Carew. 'Nothing happened, your ex didn't have a pop at you and no police showed up. Have we got the right place? Is this the Deryn Du?'

'You saw the sign outside, didn't you?' said the woman.

'I'd like a word with your ex.'

'He's not here.'

'You surprise me. All right – what's his name and where can I find him?'

'His name's Seán. Seán Tyrone. You might find him up at the hall.'

Carew took a card from his wallet and placed it on the bar.

'If you change your mind or remember anything you haven't told us, this is my number. Anything you choose to say will be treated with the strictest confidence; you have my personal assurance of that.'

'I've got nothing to tell you because there's nothing to tell.'

'How about you, Grandpa?'

'I'll have a half if you're buying,' said the old man.

'If you do find the cowing scumbag,' said the woman, 'lock him up and throw away the bastard key.'

'Why? What's he done?'

'Make something up. You're good at that.'

'Come on, Crowther. Let's get some fresh air.'

Outside, Carew lit a cigarette.

'They're lying of course,' said Crowther.

'Tell me something new. Know any jokes?'

'Here's one now.'

He nodded over Carew's shoulder. Carew turned and saw Fat Edwards coming up the street.

'What the hell are you doing here?' said Carew. 'Two o'clock we said. And where's Bald Edwards?'

'Don't know. I've looked all over. I thought he might have come here.'

'You were supposed to stick together.'

'I know,' said Fat Edwards. 'But we thought we'd get the job done faster if we split up like.'

Carew sighed and threw down his cigarette butt.

'You'd better wait here and see if he turns up at two. And you're on Coke, mind. Better make it Diet.'

Carew and Crowther walked up the hill until they came to the top of the village.

'According to the map,' said Crowther, 'Parry Hall is on the other side of this wood.'

As they took the path, tarmac soon gave way to gravel and then to flattened earth. The trees advanced on either side until the two men were forced to walk in single file. Crowther halted.

'Hang on a minute. I need a waz.'

Carew nodded curtly and Crowther went behind the trees. Carew took out a cigarette. That woman in the pub. How could they let themselves go like that? If she'd bother to take any pride in her appearance she'd probably scrub up quite well. He wouldn't kick her out of bed.

'Come on, man. What are you doing in there? Put your dick away and give it the rest of the day off. Crowther?'

Carew entered the wood and followed the trail of flattened fern, calling out his colleague's name at intervals with increasing irritation. Decaying undergrowth took over from the ferns, leaving no clue as to Crowther's progress. A crow observed him from an upper branch and croaked its encouragement. Carew swore at the bird and pressed on, thorns tugging at his sleeves.

The crow reappeared in a tree ahead and croaked again before flying a short distance to alight on another branch. It looked at Carew expectantly. For no reason, Carew felt he should follow and went with his instinct. For ten minutes or more he trusted in his guide, even after it occurred to him that he had no sense of the way back to the path. Eventually the crow settled on a bough and cawed with what appeared in Carew's imagination to be a note of finality. Carew emerged into a clearing.

Five policemen, four in uniform, sat in a circle each with his back to a tree. Crowther, Kendrick, Morris, Fat Edwards, Bald Edwards.

'What the hell's this? The teddy bears' bloody picnic? On your feet, the lot of you. Bunch of sodding layabouts. You're all on a charge. Stand up.'

A noose closed around his neck. As the garotte tightened he was aware of a soft Irish brogue at his ear.

'I'm sure they'd like to oblige, sir. But they're all dead.'

Seán Tyrone dragged the corpse across the clearing and carefully positioned it against a tree, closing the circle. Then he made his way home, a policeman's helmet perched jauntily on his head.

Descent and Ascension

Our heroes stand, hewn out in stone
Alabaster forms their thighs
King David on his marble throne –
Who dares to meet those rock-hard eyes?

We're told that we should strive to be
Heroic in our little way,
And imitate this statuary
We mortals with our feet of clay.

Lewis ap Bwgan

I stood in the cage gripping the sides for balance. Jimmy had lent me a helmet with a lamp attached. I was grateful for the light but I anticipated the helmet would afford me no more protection from whatever demons I might encounter than the cross that hung around my neck or the pistol that lay in my pocket.

Down down to the depths of the earth, rattling and riddling in the dark dark dark, shaking and shivering until I hit the ground – down to the underground to the depths of the earth no light no air no life shaking and shivering in that black underground.

At pit bottom I left the cage. My legs were unsteady supports but I called out into the darkness.

'Father? It's Jack. Your son, Jack. Are you there?'

The lamp on my helmet began to flicker. I tapped it a couple of times and it went out.

But there shining in its own luminosity was a pile of bones. The skull grinned and I saw the glint of a gold tooth. I knew at once this was my father, Seán Tyrone.

Then the skull spoke.

'So Jack, my old lad. You've come to pay me a visit after all these years. How's your mother? She must be getting on a bit now and I wouldn't have thought time's treated her all that kindly.'

Better than it's treated you by the looks of things, I think, but say nothing. But wait. Can he hear what I'm thinking? If the voice is in my head as it must be, then surely he must be aware of everything else that's going on in there. Then I'd better be careful of what I'm thinking. But how do you go about doing that? And how can I stop thinking about how to stop thinking about it? Oh, what the hell…

'I always had it in mind to drop the pair of you a line to let you know how I was doing – maybe even send for you but things kind of got on top of me what with one thing and another and in the end, to tell you the truth, I couldn't be arsed. You know how it is.'

I do now.

'And how's yourself? I see you've grown into a fine figure of a young man, a regular chip off the old block. I'll lay odds you're a regular devil with the ladies by now, isn't that the truth? Come on, you can be open with your old man.'

'I'm not a chip off any old block. I'm my own man. Jack O'Brien. I may be cursed with your blood in my veins but I'll be damned if I carry any other part of you.'

I took the pistol from my pocket and threw it down among the bones.

'You can take this stinking tool of death for a start. Life may be cheap and sorry to your way of thinking but the blood of another human creature will never stain these hands. And this locket. Do you know that my mother has worn it around her neck all these years for love of you? For the love of a dirty thief and murderer who never gave a moment's thought to her or the child he'd left her to bring up alone? But what can you understand about love? All that has driven you has been your loathsome appetite. Tell me about love, father. Pass on your wisdom. Come on, your son is eager to learn.'

The skull was silent if ever it had spoken. The lamp on my helmet flickered back into life and I leant down to hang my mother's locket around my father's neck.

'Goodbye, Seán Tyrone.'

It was now that I noticed the pool of water in which I stood. It was not still as a puddle is, but appeared to be flowing gently down the tunnel. The lamp could give no clue as to its source but the lapping at my boots grew in intensity and the level was perceptibly rising. Now it was at my ankles. A beam cracked above my head, and I looked up. A shower of earth fell into my eyes and before I could clear them I was aware of water entering the tops of my boots. From further down the tunnel came muffled explosions as timbers buckled and gave way. Now the water was at my knees; I waded through it with painful effort until I reached the cage. Once inside my prison I rang the bell. There was no response so I rang again, panic twisting in my guts and rising in my throat as I rang again and again and again. I saw the props bend and crack, the earth spill from the roof, the debris smash at the cage and all the time the water was rising, rising.

Through all that hellish noise I became aware of the machinery struggling to life above my head. I begged with all my will for its success and was rewarded as the cage begain to lift from the ground and suck itself from the infernal mire. Once free it began to accelerate, shaking and shuddering in rage and anger, but such was my relief at having been rescued I felt only gratitude to this machine and its eccentricities. At last I was belched on to land but this was no terra firma. The ground rolled and rumbled beneath my sodden feet. In the row of houses across the street, windows splintered and burst as the walls pitched on their uncertain foundations. Cracks shot up in the brickwork and chimneys crashed on to the pavement. At the top of the village I saw houses swallowed up by the ground two and three at a time and a river of slag began to course down the main throughway gathering everything in its path. Now the walls opposite fell and patterned wallpapers hung with pictures in frames were revealed to me briefly before they too fell into the wreckage.

But in all this carnage there was no sign of any human presence.

I had to tear my dreadful fascination from this awesome sight and look to my own salvation. Behind the colliery lay the railway track, long disused but still navigable and so ran to it just as the street on which I had been standing subsided into the ground with a great roar of mortal defiance. Nor did I stop running until blinded by the blood my tortured heart had forced behind my eyes. I fell to the track, lungs goaded beyond endurance, immobile save for the palsied shaking of my hands as they gripped incontinently at the gravel beneath the rails.

When I was able to regain my feet I looked back at Aberuffern but it had gone; only the woods remained. I turned and walked down the track. Dawn was breaking and I was going home to bury my mother.

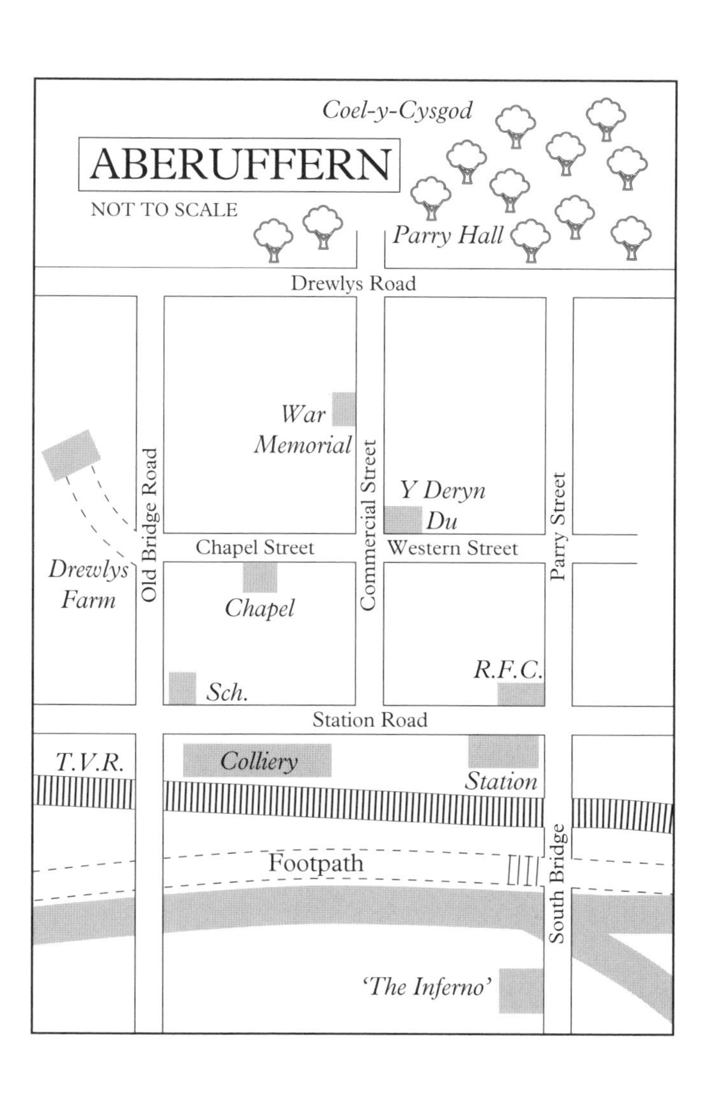
Coel-y-Cysgod
ABERUFFERN
NOT TO SCALE
Parry Hall
Drewlys Road
War
Memorial
Y Deryn
Du
Old Bridge Road
Commercial Street
Parry Street
Chapel Street
Western Street
Drewlys
Farm
Chapel
R.F.C.
Sch.
Station Road
T.V.R.
Colliery
Station
Footpath
South Bridge
'The Inferno'

About the Author

Mark Ryan was born in London in 1959. After leaving school at sixteen he toured in various bands including Adam and the Ants and appeared in Derek Jarman's 1977 film *Jubilee*. In the late 1980s he attended Dartington College of Arts and gained a degree in music, collaborating with the theatre department on a wide range of productions. Mark moved to Wales in 1991, settling in Cardiff where he worked in professional theatre as a playwright, musician and designer.

He was a prolific playwright producing work that often integrated music and song with vibrant dialogue. His work reached a wide audience including children and young people, winning acclaim and awards. *The Strange Case of Dr Jekyll and Mr Hyde as told to Carl Jung by an inmate of Broadmoor Asylum* was first performed at the Edinburgh Festival in 1997 and was *The Scotsman*'s Five Star, Pick of The Day; while *The Lazy Ant*, a play for four to seven year olds, won Best Script and Best Production at the International Children's Theatre Festival in Shanghai in 2007.

Seán Tyrone was originally a play, first performed in 2010, and is an exploration of Jack O'Brien's quest for identity after his mother sends him to Wales to seek his errant father. In this novelisation, Mark uses his skills as an artist to illustrate the story with original woodcuts, interweaving it with a cast of colourful characters. Mark died in 2011 while finalising the text for the novel.